LEFT FOR DEAD

LEFT FOR DEAD

LEFT FOR DEAD

Dead For Good Book Two

STACY CLAFLIN

NOLON KING

STERLING & STONE

Chapter One

BRAD MORRIS GLANCED around the packed sanctuary, pretending to watch the slideshow of his neighbor's life. Beside him, his wife sniffled. He put his arm around her and kissed her cheek.

Several of the other funeral guests looked away as his gaze met theirs.

Just like with the murder of his next-door neighbor, people were eyeing him with suspicion. It was ridiculous. Why would he kill any of his neighbors? Even if they'd known he was an assassin — which they didn't — it still wouldn't make sense. He killed the bad guys. Not people who merely annoyed him.

There was no denying that both Duke and Allison had annoyed him. He hadn't made any secret of that fact. But that didn't mean he wanted either of them dead.

Brad only wanted to rid the world of serial murderers, rapists, terrorists, and the like. Those were the people he took out, and only when assigned to him.

But he couldn't explain that to his neighbors. Or to the police. The only person who knew the real nature of his job was his wife, Faye, and she'd only recently learned the truth.

The slideshow ended, and Allison's teenage son Nate stood behind the pulpit. Cleared his throat loudly into the mic, making the speaker screech.

He apologized, his cheeks reddening, and thanked everyone for coming. Then shared a story about his mom staying up all night to make a Halloween costume for him one year when he'd changed his mind about what he wanted to be last-minute.

When the teenager's voice caught, and he wiped tears from his eyes, a lump formed in Brad's own throat, and he blinked back tears of his own.

He wasn't the only one. Sniffles sounded around him.

After Nate finished, his dad took his place behind the podium. Wes shared a few more stories about his wife before the preacher said a prayer and invited everyone downstairs for food and fellowship.

Zeke tugged on Brad's jacket. "Can we go?"

Brad shook his head at his fourteen-year-old.

Zeke frowned but nodded.

Allison had been Faye's friend, so they were all expected to stay for a while. Brad was as eager to leave as his son, but at the same time, he wanted to take advantage of the time to look around for the real killer.

It had taken the police too long to find Duke's killer, and as a result, almost everyone in the neighborhood thought it was Brad because he'd been the only one to openly dislike the guy. Though, as he learned more about his neighbors, he'd found others.

But if people knew the truth about his daughter, they'd still suspect him despite the true killer being behind bars.

Brad helped Faye to her feet, and as a family, all five of them headed downstairs, mournfully greeting the other guests. Luna clung to Brad's hand, sticking close. Faye worried that she'd be too young for a memorial service, but Brad had assured her that seven was plenty old enough. And he'd been right. Others brought children even younger than her.

Downstairs, they got in the buffet line. Brad glanced around for anyone out of place. No one stood out, but chances were, the killer was here. Watching. Reveling in his accomplishment. It wasn't the same as returning to the scene of the crime, but close enough.

That wouldn't last long. Brad would make sure of it. Someone was framing him. Killing off people who annoyed him.

But the question was, why?

Figuring that out would lead him to the who.

"Can you help Luna?" Faye asked.

"Of course." He gave his wife a reassuring smile before helping their youngest pile food on her plate.

Soon the three of them were sitting at a table — Zeke and Hadley had joined their respective friends.

Faye turned to Luna. "Do you have any questions?"

"About what?" She bit into a miniature sandwich.

"The service. Or Allison passing away."

"You mean dying." Luna frowned. "It's sad. I liked the stories her kids shared. The camping one was funny."

Brad smiled. "It was. At least her family has all those memories to hold onto. They'll never forget her."

"Just like with grandpa." Luna looked deep in thought. "You told me all those stories about him. Sometimes I forget I never met him."

Brad kissed the top of her head, the lump in his throat returning.

Faye leaned over. "So, you're okay with being here?"

"Yeah. I liked watching the pictures."

Brad squeezed her knee and thought back to his own childhood, to his dad's murder when he was only sixteen. "It's all good. Kids can handle more than adults give them credit for." He glanced at Luna. "Right?"

"Yep." She smiled, showing off her missing teeth, and gulped her drink.

Faye set her fork down on her nearly full plate. "I'm going to give my condolences to Wes. Do you want to join me?"

Just the man's name made Brad's stomach turn, but he forced a smile. "Sure."

She gave him an appreciative glance. "Thank you."

"Can I get a cookie?" Luna asked. "Please?"

"You can have two." Brad winked.

Her expression lit up, and she scrambled out of her chair.

Brad laced his fingers through Faye's as they made their way to Allison's husband. He shoved aside thoughts of past offenses and offered heartfelt sympathy to the man who'd just lost his wife so violently.

Faye gave him a hearty hug and told him how much she was going to miss Allison.

Someone tapped Brad on the shoulder.

He turned to see his boss, Kurt Bergmann. "I didn't expect to see you here."

Kurt motioned toward an empty table.

Brad nodded and let Faye know he was going to talk with Kurt.

"What's going on?" Brad sat next to him. "Is something wrong?"

Kurt shook his head, his expression unreadable. "I thought someone from BlueBlade should be here to offer you support. Do you need anything?"

"Other than for someone to stop framing me for murder?"

A corner of Kurt's mouth curved up. "Yes, other than that. Do you have any idea who that might be?"

"No."

Kurt panned the room with his palm. "The person must be here."

"My thoughts exactly."

Kurt leaned closer. "If you need anything, just say the word. My resources are your resources."

Brad covered his surprise. When everyone was pointing fingers at him from Duke's murder, Kurt had disappeared. Given him nothing.

Now he was here at the funeral, offering everything.

"Just let me know." Kurt looked at the time. "I need to get going. You've got my number."

And Brad's calls would likely just go to voicemail as they had in the past. Kurt just wanted to make sure Brad kept BlueBlade out of the investigation.

"Right."

Kurt left.

Faye came over and put her hands on his shoulders. "What was that about?"

"Offering his support, but I'm not going to hold my breath."

"I wouldn't worry about people suspecting you for this. You were at the party the whole time — everyone saw you." She gave him a quick kiss. "I'm going to check on Luna. Looks like she took a whole pile of cookies."

Brad started to smile, but then Detective Stewart entered the room, her presence as welcoming as a black hole.

She locked gazes with him and marched his way.

Of course.

He squeezed Faye's hand as she strolled away, then rose to meet her. "Detective Stewart."

She shook his hand. "Mr. Morris."

"Any leads on the killer?"

"You know I can't discuss an open investigation. I do have a few questions for you. Have a moment?"

"Sure." He plopped back into his seat, his stomach knotting. "Ask away."

"I'm curious about your knife collection."

Allison had been stabbed. So had her fake pregnant belly. Shredded by her murderer.

"Brad?"

He turned his attention back to the detective. "You have all of my Valderdorfs, remember? You needed them for Duke's investigation."

"Right, but again, every time I ask your neighbors about Allison's enemies, your name comes up."

Brad squeezed his fists under the table but managed to keep his expression relaxed. "We weren't enemies. She kept coming to my house and accusing me of murder. I don't imagine you'd take too kindly to that treatment, either."

"You don't have any other Valderdorfs?"

"No. Is that what was used on Allison?"

She held his gaze. "What other knives do you have?"

"Too many to list. Although I'm beginning to think that cataloging them would be a good idea."

"I don't need a full list. Can you tell me the ones that come to your mind?"

He held back an annoyed sigh before listing off the BlueBlade models that he could think of at the moment.

"Slow down." She held up a hand. "I can't write that fast."

"Maybe you'd prefer I email you the list." He leaned back and put his hands behind his head to let the onlookers know he wasn't upset. Just having a conversation with the police detective. Nothing interesting there.

She glared at him. "If your collection is that vast, maybe it would be a good idea."

"Great. I'll get right on that."

"I'm sure you will." She rose and gave him a card to add to his stack at home. "I'll be in touch. Let me know if you think of anything useful."

"Will do."

The detective left without another word.

Brad got up and gave an easy smile to the nearest table of onlookers. Then he went into the hallway for some air. The quiet wrapped around him like a warm blanket.

Being around all those suspicious stares was too much. He paced, taking measured breaths. He could get through the remainder of the reception. With any luck, he could convince Faye to leave before too long. But even if not, it would give him the opportunity to look around for a guilty party.

Even his boss thought the murderer would be there.

He started for the door when sniffling sounded. Someone blew their nose.

Brad followed the noise.

Nate cowered in a darkened hallway, his face buried in a tissue. He looked more like a little boy than a young man about to graduate high school and play football for the Huskies.

Brad backed away to give him space. "Are you okay?"

Nate looked up, his eyes bloodshot. "What do you want?"

"Just checking on you. Do you need anything?"

"Not from you." He turned away and blew his nose.

Brad knelt and rested a hand on his shoulder. "I know what it feels like."

"No, you don't."

"My father was murdered when I was a little younger than you."

Nate gave him a double-take. "He was?"

Brad nodded. "I thought it would kill me."

"How'd you deal with it?" Nate wiped his eyes.

"It wasn't easy." Brad leaned against the wall and sat next to him. "I had to rely on my mom and Faye. If it weren't for them, I don't know how I would've managed."

"You knew Faye back then?"

"Yeah. We've been together since high school."

"How did you—?"

Wes stepped into the hallway, glaring at Nate. "There you are. You need to get back in there. People are asking about you." He turned to Brad. "What are you doing?"

"Offering some advice, from one child of a murdered parent to another."

"I'll be the one to give my son guidance. You can mind your own business." Wes helped his son up, and as they left, Nate glanced back, giving Brad a look of appreciation.

As Brad stood, he studied Wes.

Had *he* been at the party when his wife was murdered? Or could he have snuck out and in again before her body had been found?

Chapter Two

FAYE COVERED Luna's ears and turned to the therapist. "We're not discussing *all* of our issues in family counseling. Just those that involve everyone."

"Understood." Dr. Trellis gave a reassuring smile. "I didn't realize *that* was off-limits."

Faye breathed a sigh of relief. It was a balancing act keeping certain secrets from other family members. They all had their right to privacy, but at the same time, all of their issues affected everyone else, whether they knew about them or not.

"What were you going to say?" Zeke looked back and forth between the therapist and Faye.

"Don't worry about it, honey. Let's focus on how we deal with grief."

Zeke frowned. "That's what we've been talking about every week. Even in my personal sessions."

Dr. Trellis leaned forward. "What do *you* want to talk about, Zeke?"

"You really want to know?"

"Why wouldn't I?"

Zeke glanced at Faye and Brad before answering. "People don't usually care about what I think."

"By people," Dr. Trellis said, "do you mean your parents?"

"I mean everyone. Family, kids at school, kids in the neighborhood. The only ones who listen to me are my friends in the game. Nobody else takes me seriously."

Faye's stomach knotted. "We take you seriously."

Dr. Trellis held up a hand. "It's his turn to talk."

Faye looked at Brad, who shrugged as if to say, *you're the one who wanted family therapy.*

"Why do you feel like people don't take you seriously?" Dr. Trellis asked Zeke.

He toyed with his wild curls. "I just don't."

"That isn't an answer."

Zeke sighed dramatically, looking around the room before turning back to the doctor. "I'm a dork. I get that. And I'm not going to change who I am, but that doesn't mean I'm not smart or that I don't have good ideas. Just because I don't get straight A's and land the lead in every school play like some people" — he glared at Hadley — "or I'm not little and cute, or I'm not an adult yet. I matter, too."

Faye leaned toward him, a lump forming in her throat. "Of course you do!"

Dr. Trellis ignored her. "Do you feel looked over as the middle child?"

"Yeah."

"And that's why you wanted to hide your friendship with Duke?"

Zeke shrugged. "I wouldn't really call it a *friendship*."

"But you went to him when you needed advice about dealing with kids at school? With your parents?"

Brad couldn't believe it. "You got advice from him about us?"

Zeke stared at his shoes. "He was the only one who took me seriously. When I asked about bullies or about how to talk to you guys, he always had some story about dealing with his parents or people giving him a hard time."

"Are you saying I give you a hard time?" Brad asked.

"That isn't what he said," Dr. Trellis said. "Let him finish."

Brad leaned back, his mouth forming a straight line.

Zeke picked at his shirt with a scene from *The Never-Ending Story* across the front. "I'm done."

Hadley turned toward him. "You have to admit that you make it hard for people to take you seriously. I mean, between your hair, your goofiness, and your 80s obsession—"

"Shut up!" Zeke's face reddened. "I already said I'm not going to change!"

"Nobody's asking you to," Dr. Trellis said.

"She is!"

"Hadley's explaining why it's hard for *her* to take you seriously."

"And the rest of the world," Hadley muttered.

Zeke crossed his arms.

Hadley flipped her long hair behind her shoulder. "If you don't want to be treated like a dork, don't act like one."

Faye glared at her daughter. "Hadley, stop."

Dr. Trellis turned to Hadley. "Does it bother you that he looks the way he does?"

"Are you kidding?"

"Do you feel he reflects on you?"

Hadley turned to her brother. "That's exactly it. My friends make fun of *me* because of the things you do. It's

11

horrifying. I work so hard to build my reputation, just to have you sabotage it."

"I don't even go to the same school as you."

"People still talk."

"And you think people don't compare me to you?" Zeke snapped. "There's no way I can live up to little miss perfect! I can't, so I don't bother. I can't help that we get compared to each other."

Faye struggled to keep up, her heart pounding. She'd had no idea either of her kids felt that way about each other. "How can we stop this?"

Dr. Trellis's timer dinged.

She turned it off. "That's all for today's session."

Just as they were beginning to get somewhere.

The doctor looked back and forth between the two teens. "In the meantime, I want you two to journal your thoughts and feelings. We'll discuss this further in your personal sessions, then again when we all come together next."

Faye stood. "What about the grief counseling? I thought we were going to talk about that. We've had two neighbors killed. People we were friends with. We—"

"There are a lot of issues that need our attention, and they're all intertwined. Oh, that reminds me. I want you to consider planning a family vacation."

"A vacation!" Luna jumped up and down, her eyes wide.

Dr. Trellis smiled. "Yes. It would do you all a world of good to get away from everything and spend some time together. I'm not talking about a trip to a theme park where every moment is packed with activity. What you need is a relaxing, pressure-free week together, perhaps on a tropical beach or at a cabin in the woods. You have access to one of those, right?"

Faye's stomach dropped at the mention of her parents' cabin. The one she and Brad had lied about being at during the time of Duke's death. "Right."

"It doesn't have to be expensive, or even for a full week. But it does need to be away from everything else for a few solid days, minimum."

Luna grabbed Faye's hand. "Let's go to the beach, Mommy!"

Faye forced a smile. "Daddy and I will have to talk about it, sweetie."

Brad headed for the door.

Dr. Trellis stopped him. "You and Faye are next, remember?"

"Oh. Right."

Faye kissed each of the kids. "We'll see you at home."

Dr. Trellis checked her calendar. "And the kids will be back next week for their appointments."

"Yes." Faye turned to Hadley. "Drive safe."

"Of course she will," Zeke said. "She's perfect, remember?"

Hadley snorted. "You don't know what you're talking about."

Faye gave her daughter a knowing glance. Only she and Brad knew Hadley's secret. It would likely take *years* of counseling before she'd be ready to tell anyone else. And the only reason she or Brad knew was that they'd accidentally stumbled upon the evidence.

The kids left the office, Zeke and Hadley grumbling at each other while Luna told them to be nice.

Faye sighed. "I hope they'll be okay."

"They will. They're good kids." Dr. Trellis sat back on her chair and motioned for her and Brad to sit across from her. "How do you feel about the idea of a family vacation?"

Brad plopped down. "Sounds great, but it'll take some time to plan. And I'll have to figure out when I can get time off."

Faye sat next to him. "And it might be tricky if I'm starting a home salon."

"Are you planning on doing that soon?" Dr. Trellis turned to Brad. "You feel good about that?"

"I don't mind a vacation if I can get away from work."

He was deflecting, Faye noticed. He still didn't want to talk about having her clients at home.

Dr. Trellis let him get away with it this time. "Is the knife business busy this time of year?"

Faye exchanged a look with Brad. They were being completely open with their therapist about everything except that Brad was secretly an assassin.

An assassin.

Her husband killed people for a living. That was the real reason they had the nice things they did.

That was something Faye could really use counseling for. But it was something she wasn't even supposed to know about. His organization was so high-level in the government that the police didn't — and couldn't — know about it. She'd just found out, and it was as hard to deal with as Brad's long-ago emotional relationship — he wouldn't let her call it an emotional affair — with Jessica.

Even though that was what it had been.

"Faye?" Dr. Trellis's voice brought her back to the office.

"Sorry. What did you say?"

"Have you thought about Rose this week?"

"Not until now." Bile rose in her mouth. She wanted to add a sarcastic *thanks* but managed to stay silent.

"Wonderful." The therapist smiled. "That's progress."

Faye shrugged. "I've been busy."

"But you haven't been worried about Brad's relationship with her."

"*Fake* relationship," Brad said quickly. "I had to lie about it to the police to keep Faye out of it."

"Out of thinking, she was involved with his murder?"

"Correct."

Dr. Trellis paused before continuing. "And you haven't had any contact with her?"

"Why would I?"

"I'm just asking a question. Yes or no?"

"No."

"Good. And you haven't been worrying about Duke?"

"Why would I worry about him? He's dead."

"Yes, but almost all of your family members felt that they had to go behind your back to be friends with him."

"Not friends," Faye clarified. "He was a client."

"Who you gave a trim to in your home hours before his death." Dr. Trellis gave her a knowing look.

"I didn't know he was going to be killed that night."

"But you lied to the police so Brad wouldn't know that you cut his hair."

Faye clenched her jaw. "So that the detective wouldn't know he was over right before his murder."

"And also so Brad wouldn't know he had been over." It wasn't a question.

"Correct," Faye said through gritted teeth. "But everything is out in the open now."

Brad put his arm around her. "No more secrets."

Faye leaned her head against his, jaw still clenched. "Exactly."

Dr. Trellis leaned forward. "Good. And you both have been journaling? Discussing your feelings with one another?"

They both nodded.

STACY CLAFLIN & NOLON KING

"How do you feel about how that's been going? Any issues you need to bring up?"

Faye glanced at Brad.

He shook his head. "It's all good."

"I agree."

"That's great news. How are you coping with Allison's death? Did the memorial service offer closure?"

Faye took a deep breath and thought about it. "I still feel guilty about letting her walk to her house alone. If I'd been there, I could've stopped the murder."

"Or you could've gotten killed, too." Brad crossed his arms.

"Two against one."

"We don't know how many people killed her. And the killer could've gone after you instead."

Dr. Trellis held up a hand. "Survivor's guilt is real, and it can haunt people for a lifetime if not dealt with properly."

"Understood." Brad turned to Faye. "I wasn't trying to discount how you feel. I just don't want to think about anything happening to you. It would kill me to lose you."

Faye's heart warmed, and she threw her arms around him.

He squeezed her, the faint scent of the cologne he'd worn since they were teenagers bringing her back to simpler days. "I love you."

"I love you, too." Faye clung to him for another moment before letting go and turning back to the therapist.

Dr. Trellis smiled. "I'm proud of the progress you're making. Now let's discuss your vacation. I'd like to set some ground rules."

What Faye really wanted to talk about was her husband, the assassin.

But she was pretty sure that doctor-patient confidentiality didn't stretch that far.

She'd have to find a way to deal with it on her own.

Chapter Three

BRAD UNPACKED and sorted the knives, but he was paying more attention to Kurt's door. On the other side, the detective was questioning his boss.

It was enough to make him break out into a cold sweat. But he kept himself together. The employees who had come into the back room hadn't given him a second glance. But he would definitely need a moment to collect himself once Detective Stewart finally left.

What was she asking him? It was taking so long.

And Kurt's words kept ringing through his head. Brad was supposed to keep the cops away from BlueBlade. But that *had* been a different investigation. That was when Brad was a suspect in Duke's murder. This was a separate murder.

Probably. Maybe. Not likely. It was too close to the other one to be a coincidence. And Brad was the only thread tying them together. Someone was framing him. He couldn't blame his neighbors for being suspicious. Not that he was happy about it.

And Kurt was going to be furious once the detective

left. He had to be silently seething right then.

Brad glanced at the clock. The second hand was barely moving. The minute hand *hadn't* moved since he'd last looked. And that felt like twenty minutes.

He sighed and turned his attention back to the new inventory. At the bottom of the box sat a Valderdorf in a special edition package.

Brad's stomach knotted. That was the type of knife that killed Duke, and also why Detective Stewart had all of Brad's — still. Even though Rose was in jail awaiting trial for the murder.

He left the last knife in the box and set it aside. No sense in giving Stewart a reason to stop and question him after leaving Kurt's office. Then he organized the other knives by type and moved to the next box.

Paused.

Glanced at the door again.

He was down to only two more boxes of new inventory, which meant one of those had the *real* inventory — information on more hits for the assassins to take down and weapons that would never see the showroom light on the other side of the employee door to the shop.

Kurt's voice sounded from his office. He had to be next to the door, ready to open it.

Relief flooded Brad. Then his pulse pounded.

Stewart would want to talk to him. But he had the advantage this time. It wasn't like with Duke's investigation. Brad had been at his own home with a house full of party guests. He hadn't been on a kill at the time of the murder. He wasn't covering for some crazy lie his wife spewed out in a moment of stress.

He was in control as usual.

Everything would be fine. Sure, he killed people. Sanctioned killings. Not random murders of innocent people.

STACY CLAFLIN & NOLON KING

Allison's death had nothing to do with him. It should take almost no effort to convince the detective of that much.

Kurt may have already done as much.

The doorknob jiggled, then the door slowly creaked open.

Brad's breath hitched. Even if the detective didn't speak with him, Kurt was going to be pissed. Brad just needed to calm him down, assure him everything was under control.

It wasn't, not yet, but he could convince Kurt easily enough.

The detective and Brad's boss exited the office. Kurt laughed as Stewart stepped out, making a note on her tablet before placing it in her pocket. Laughing was a good sign. Unless he was covering his fury. It could go either way.

Brad turned away from them, whipped out a pocketknife, and slowly cut open the next box. The real inventory would be at the bottom. Even if it was in this particular box, the detective wouldn't see anything suspicious. Not if Brad was deliberative, took his time.

Detective Stewart's heels echoed around the back room as she made her way toward the main part of the store. She didn't even glance Brad's way before turning the knob and leaving.

Kurt, however, waved him in.

Brad's stomach knotted, but he stood taller and marched in like he owned the place. "How'd that go?"

"Have a seat." Kurt motioned to the chair on the other side of his desk and opened his mini-fridge. "Did you have anything to do with your neighbor's murder?"

"We've been over this."

"And now your detective is questioning me. We're going over it again."

"*My* detective?"

"She sure isn't mine." Kurt turned around, two expensive beers in his hands, and handed one to Brad before collapsing onto his chair.

Brad looked back and forth between the drink and Kurt, throwing him a questioning glance.

His boss opened his drink and tossed the opener to Brad.

He caught it and loosened the cap.

Kurt took a long swig of his beer. "That's better." He motioned for Brad to have a drink. "It's a special edition I picked up the last time I went to Cameroon."

Brad tried some. It went down smoother than expected, helped him to relax. "It's good."

"It's better than good." Kurt took another long sip.

Brad followed suit, his nerves getting the best of him despite the drink relaxing him. Kurt had never offered him a drink from his special stash before.

Something was up.

He couldn't stand the silence a moment longer. "Did the detective give you a hard time?"

"Just doing her job. I mean, really, what can we expect when someone killed one of your neighbors with a Valderdorf?"

"Allison's murderer used one, too?" Brad sat up straighter.

"No, not her. Your other neighbor. The first one."

"I knew that. But Allison was also killed with a knife. Detective Stewart wouldn't tell me what kind."

Kurt emptied his bottle and set it down. "She was more interested in the knives you own."

"She already has all of my Valderdorfs. Does she want everything else?"

"Probably. The way she was talking, you'd think I kept

detailed records on everything my employees own. Like I have time for that." He laughed.

Brad forced a laugh.

Kurt leaned forward and held Brad's gaze. "That woman has it out for you. We need to get her attention somewhere else."

"We?"

"Yes. Can't have her poking around here. Especially not when we're getting new inventory."

"My thoughts exactly."

Kurt leaned back. "Thoughts on how we're going to do that?"

Brad took a sip of his beer to give him a moment to think. "I'm already looking for actual suspects."

"Have you looked at the woman's husband? He seems squirrelly if you ask me."

"He's more than squirrelly."

"Meaning?"

"The guy tried to make my wife think I was having an affair with Rose."

Kurt tapped his desk. "Covering for his own actions."

"You think he was having an affair on Allison?"

"I never saw them together. What do *you* think?"

Brad tried to remember who Wes had been with at the bar when he'd made sure Allison told Faye about Brad running into Rose at the bar. He was pretty sure he'd been with some other guys from the neighborhood. Brad hadn't been paying that close of attention, given everything else going on at the time. "I wouldn't put it past him."

"You're going to need to focus on him. Was he at your party when the chick was killed?"

"That's what I've been trying to remember. I was talking to someone else at the time. Really wasn't paying Wes any attention."

"So, you're already considering him."

Brad nodded and finished off his drink, resting his elbow on the desk. He felt a lot better than when he'd entered the office.

"Here's what I think." Kurt flipped through some papers. "I give you some personal time off. We'll say you're working on the website from home — I'll update a few things to make it seem legit. Use that to look into the case. Figure out who killed that woman so your detective will get her focus off us."

Brad's elbow slid off the desk. He recovered quickly and sat up straight. "You're laying me off?"

"It's a cover. Your time is better spent getting that chick off our backs. I'll get Bill to finish the inventory."

"What about my assignments?"

"Oh, you're still going to kill them. You just won't be coming *here* Monday through Friday."

Brad nodded. "Understood."

"Clear some things from your locker and tell Lauren about your new working-from-home routine. Once she knows, everyone else will, too. Then we can focus on what's really important."

Brad rose. "How often do you want me checking in?"

"As necessary." He patted his pocket. "My phone's on."

As opposed to last time, but Brad kept that thought to himself. "Sounds good. I'll be in touch."

Kurt turned his attention to his computer. "I'm not worried."

Brad's mind raced as he made his way to his locker. It was beyond weird that his boss had done a 180. During the investigation of Duke's murder, he couldn't reach the man. Now he was giving him expensive beer and letting him have some time off.

It didn't make sense. But now, he had plenty of time to figure out what was going on.

The only problem with him working from home was that it didn't give him the opportunity to look into the other employees. While it stood to reason that Rose could be innocent — if someone was framing him for both murders, it couldn't be her. She'd been in jail when Allison was killed. If the person setting him up worked at Blue-Blade, he needed to figure that out, too.

Rose had been friends with all the employees, so it could be anyone.

In the meantime, if he managed to eliminate all of his neighbors, he would convince Kurt to let him come back to work, and he could figure out who was after him if it was someone here.

Lauren came in from the shop, grabbed her sack lunch from her locker, and sat at the table.

Brad made a production of grabbing an empty box and piling his things inside.

She lifted a brow. "What are you doing?"

"Nothing."

Lauren set her sandwich down. "Looks like you're emptying your locker. That isn't nothing."

He set the box next to her food with a thud. "I'm going to be working from home on the website for a little while. It's no big deal."

Her eyes widened. "Did Kurt demote you?"

Brad covered a smile. It was too easy raising her curiosity. "Not at all. I took some computer programming classes in college, so he wants me to update the site. You could think of it as a promotion."

She studied him. "Really?"

He turned back to his locker and pulled out a few stray

items he'd forgotten about. "Yep. I also have a lot going on personally, so it works out."

"You mean the investigation?" She scooted her chair closer. "I saw that detective come in. She was back here a long time. Did she interrogate you?"

Brad snorted. "No. Just asked Kurt a few questions about our knives."

"She didn't even talk to you?"

"Nope." He grabbed the box.

Lauren's eyes narrowed. "The detective was in there" — she nodded toward Kurt's office — "the entire time? Asking about knives?"

"We do have a lot of knives."

"Still, that's a long time. What else were they doing in there? Was her makeup messed up when she came out?"

"Would you grow up?" Brad headed for the back door. "Enjoy your lunch."

"And you enjoy updating the website." Her tone indicated she didn't believe him.

Not that he cared.

As soon as he loaded the box into his trunk, his cell phone buzzed with a text.

He pulled it out, expecting Kurt to have additional instructions for him.

It was from Faye, and given the dancing dots, she was tapping another text. It came in before he had a chance to read the first.

Faye: Why aren't you answering your phone?

Faye: You need to call me back right away.

Another came in.

Faye: Emergency!!

Brad's breath hitched. Had something happened to one of the kids? Or was another neighbor dead?

Another text came in, but he ignored it and returned Faye's call.

"Why weren't you answering?" she exclaimed.

"My ringer was off. I was dealing with some stuff at work."

She gasped. "You weren't killing someone, were you?"

"Don't say that out loud!" His heart hammered. "And no, I wasn't. I was talking to Kurt after the detective left. What's the emergency?"

"It's your mom. She's in the hospital. We have to get there right away!"

Brad leaned against his Mercedes and gasped for air. "What happened? An accident?"

"I don't have any details. I'll meet you there."

"See you in a few." He ended the call, pulled himself together, and climbed into the driver's seat.

26

Chapter Four

HADLEY PUSHED through the small crowd of students gathered around the newly posted paper outside the school auditorium. Filled with names and roles.

Did she make the lead?

Sam Jensen threw a book on floor and stormed away, muttering.

Obviously, he didn't get the male lead. That was actually a relief, given his temper. People with tempers set hers off. So far, they had avoided being leads at the same time.

Hadley finally made it to the front. Started at the top of the page.

There was her name, right on the top line. Her heart soared. She'd done it. Two leads in a row.

Lucy threw her arms around Hadley and squeezed. "Congrats, girl! The lead again. Are you just so excited?"

Hadley beamed. "I can't believe it!"

"Sasha's gonna be so mad. Did you see her trying to outdo you at the tryouts? She was practically glowing green. I can't wait to see her reaction." Lucy glanced around. "Where is she?"

Hadley shrugged. "I don't care. I'm just glad she isn't here to ruin my mood."

"Want to celebrate? We can go to that chocolate shop and order anything we want."

"Raincheck?" Hadley grinned as she glanced at the time. Duke would just be getting home. She needed to tell him the good news.

But she couldn't. He was gone. A new family was going to move into his house soon. It had just sold.

"I just remembered something." She ran off, fighting tears.

How could she be so stupid? She knew Duke was dead, that she couldn't tell him about getting the lead role. But that didn't stop her from having moments where she forgot.

Blissful, fleeting moments when she still lived in a world with him in it.

Hadley turned down a hall and nearly crashed into someone. She knocked some papers from his hands. "I'm so sorry."

"It's all right."

Fighting back her tears, she scooped them up and handed them to him. It was Nate, Allison's son.

Their gazes locked for a moment before he spoke. "Are you okay?"

"I should be asking you that."

"I'm fine, other than having someone crash into me and mix up my papers." One corner of his mouth curved up.

"Let me fix them." She reached for the messy stack.

He pulled it away. "Don't worry about it."

"You sure?"

"Yeah. It's no problem. What has you so upset?"

She sniffled and leaned against a locker. "I just found out I made the lead role for the new school play and—"

"You're nearly in tears because of that?" He lifted a brow.

"No. I was so excited and wanted to tell D— tell someone. But then I realized he's dead and I can't." Tears blurred her vision.

"I know exactly how that feels. It sucks."

"Yeah, it does." She tried to blink back the tears, but they only spilled onto her face. "I hate this."

"Me, too. I keep wanting to tell my mom things and then I realize I can't."

She stared at him. They were going through the exact same thing. Well, not *exactly* but close enough. "I'm sorry. How are you getting through it?"

Nate glanced around before taking a step closer. "Sometimes I pretend she's with me and I tell her anyway. I know she isn't really there, but it helps. My dad thinks it's stupid, so I can't do that around him."

"Seriously?"

"Unfortunately."

"My parents have me in counseling."

He looked interested. "Does that help?"

"I guess. But nothing is going to bring him back — that's the only thing I really want."

Nate leaned against the locker next to her. "That's the part that sucks so much. I hate it more than anything. Can I ask who died?"

"Can you keep a secret?"

"I just told you that I talk to myself and my dad thinks I'm stupid for it."

Hadley's heart thundered. "My boyfriend."

Nate turned to her, confusion in his eyes. "Who was that? Not Emmett Moon?"

29

"No. He didn't go to school here." Hadley sighed. Duke was gone, and she was still covering their relationship. But now it wasn't because he could get into trouble, it was just habit. Or was she worried what people would say? People might not even believe her, and it wasn't like Duke was around to back up her story. Women in their twenties and thirties had thrown themselves at him all the time — right in front of her.

It did seem a little crazy that he would pick her, someone he had to hide from the world when he wanted to shout from the rooftops. Hadley herself had had a hard time believing at times. How could she expect anyone to believe her? She hadn't even told Ellie, and they told each other everything. Obviously not everything. Maybe someday. She did have pictures and videos for proof. She had them all memorized at this point, given how many times she'd watched them.

Nate cleared his throat, bringing her back to the present day. A life without Duke Hill.

A life that sucked.

"You wanna get burgers? We can talk about how crappy death is, or not. It's kind of nice just being with someone who gets it, even if we both get lost in our own thoughts. Or maybe I'm just rambling and being stupid."

"You aren't stupid. Don't let your dad get to you, okay? I talk to my boyfriend all the time. This is normal. Your dad's living in denial. I'll bet he's pretending she's just out somewhere and coming home soon. He's the stupid one."

Nate studied her. "So, that's a yes to burgers?"

She chuckled. "Yeah. Where do you want to go?"

They discussed the details and ten minutes later met at the greasy fast food restaurant. The aromas made her mouth water, and after realizing she hadn't eaten all day, she ordered twice her normal amount.

When they sat, Nate eyed her pile of food. "Feeding an army?"

"Don't hate on me. I skipped lunch." She took a bite of a double bacon cheeseburger. It was like a dream.

"No hate here. I'm impressed. Most girls at school won't eat more than a salad in front of guys."

"Most girls are stupid." She inhaled a bunch of fries. "I don't remember this stuff tasting so good."

He laughed. "I think it's the grief. Nothing looks or tastes the same as before."

"True." Hadley sucked down some root beer. Even that made her taste buds sing.

Nate picked at his food while she continued to scarf down hers. Even though she'd ordered twice as much as him, she finished first.

"Definitely impressed." He handed her his half-full fries. "It's yours if you want it."

"Thanks." She took it from him.

"You might want to consider not skipping lunch." His tone held a laugh to it.

"You're so right."

Nate leaned back and glanced outside. A moment later, he jolted.

"You okay?" Hadley wiped some sauce that spilled on her shirt. Why was she being such a pig in front of him? At least he didn't seem to care.

He leaned toward the window, blinking quickly. "I thought I saw my mom for a moment. It was someone else — obviously."

"I hate that."

Nate turned to her, his eyes shining. "Do you think that'll ever stop?"

"I don't know, but I like to think it'll get better at some point. Were you close to your mom?"

He nodded. "A lot closer to her than my dad. She always believed in me. I can never do anything good enough for him."

"My dad used to be like that." She crushed the empty fry container.

"Used to be?"

"He's changed a lot."

Nate looked off to the side. "What made him change?"

"Counseling."

"My dad would never go. Once he told Mom she could go because he hoped it would fix her, but said he was fine."

"What a jerk."

"Yep."

Silence settled between them. It was surprisingly comfortable, considering she and Nate had never really spent any time together before. But now they shared kind of a bond.

"Did you get to know my mom before she died?" Nate asked. "She was going over to your house a lot."

"I was busy with my play, so I only saw her in passing." The truth was, she'd been mourning Duke and barely noticed who was or wasn't in her house.

"You want to hear something crazy?" He studied her like he was gauging her reaction.

"Sure."

"My dad thinks your dad killed my mom."

Hadley frowned. It wasn't surprising, considering pretty much the whole neighborhood thought he killed Duke.

"I don't think that," Nate said quickly.

"Your dad has already proved himself stupid by the way he treats you."

"Do *you* think we have a serial killer in our midst?"

"No." Hadley finished her root beer. "Rose Flores killed Duke, and she was in jail when … you know."

"When my mom was murdered. You can say it."

Hadley looked away.

"How'd your boyfriend die?"

Now he was getting in dangerous territory.

"You don't have to talk about it."

She hesitated. "He was murdered, too."

"Seriously?" Nate's eyes nearly popped out of his head. "Three murders? Was he local? It couldn't have been around here. There weren't any killings before Duke's. Not in Pine Harbor. Used to be the safest place on the planet."

"Used to be."

"Where was your boyfriend killed?"

The ever-present lump in her throat doubled in size. "I don't want to talk about it."

"Sure, no problem. Can I ask you something?"

"You just did."

"I mean about my mom. Our moms were pretty close, right?"

"Yeah, I guess. What are you getting at?" She studied him, trying to guess.

"Does your mom have any idea who might've killed my mom? Did she tell her anything about an enemy? A jilted lover, maybe?"

Hadley choked on air. "You're accusing your dead mom of cheating on your dad?"

"I wouldn't blame her if she did. I would dad-cheat on him if I could."

"Dad cheat?"

"Go to someone else's dad and get life advice from him instead."

"That's what my brother did with Duke. I'll have to tell him there's a name for that."

"Zeke got advice from Duke?" Nate chewed on his lower lip.

"Yep. Why?"

"You're going to think I'm stupid."

She narrowed her eyes. "Stop saying that, would you? This is going to turn into a drinking game. Seriously."

He sighed, and pink colored his cheeks. "Fine. Duke gave me advice, too."

"Really?" Hadley's heart swelled. Duke really had been the best guy ever.

And now he was dead.

That thought made her want to kill Rose Flores.

Nate played with a wrapper. "Duke gave me tips on talking to a girl, but I chickened out." He looked away. "I don't know why I'm telling you all of this."

"Duke was my boyfriend," she blurted.

Both of them widened their eyes.

Hadley's heart hammered. She swore. But she also felt oddly relieved at the admission. "You can't tell anyone. Even Ellie doesn't know."

Nate's expression was unreadable.

Her stomach did flips. "Seriously, don't say anything."

"I won't." He leaned forward. "You know, I can totally see that."

"You can?"

"Yeah. It actually makes a lot of sense, especially with you telling me about your boyfriend being murdered. You two would've been the 'it' couple."

"If we could've told anyone."

He frowned, but then he relaxed. "If it makes you feel any better, he talked a lot about you when we were talking about girls. He adored you."

A slow smile spread across her face. "Thanks for telling me."

"Do you have any pictures?"

"Of him?"

"Of you two together."

"Are you kidding?" She pulled out her phone and opened her photos app, showing off some of her favorites.

Nate smiled, but then frowned. "I'm really sorry for your loss. It must suck not being able to tell anyone what you're going through."

"It does."

His phone beeped, and he looked at the screen. "Crap. I gotta go."

She glanced at the time. "Same. You promise not to tell anyone about me and Duke?"

"Of course. You promise not to tell people my dad thinks I'm stupid?"

Hadley picked up her empty cup and sucked in air. "You're supposed to stop saying that."

"Fine. But you promise?"

She held out her pinky. "Your secret is safe with me."

He looped his finger through hers. "And yours is safe with me."

As they gathered their things, Hadley felt lighter.

She actually had a friend she could talk to about Duke. Someone who understood.

Chapter Five

BRAD STARED at the blank wall of the ER waiting room, trying to take in the news of his mom's injury while simultaneously attempting to ignore all of the noise from the patients, doctors, and loudspeaker. His mom's broken arm wasn't *that* big of a deal. Probably more so at her age, but still, it could've been a lot worse.

It was the fact that the doctor thought she might have early onset dementia that had felt like a punch to the throat. She was still young and was a fun grandma to the kids. How could she be on the road to forgetting them all?

Faye squeezed his hand. "Brad?"

"Did you say something?"

She gave him a sad smile. "Are we going to be able to take her in?"

That was the other surprise. His mom couldn't return home alone. Someone needed to take care of her, and all of the facilities had waitlists a mile long according to the doctor.

He drew in a long, measured breath. "I'm going to be

working from home for a while, so it works in the short term."

Faye jolted. "Working from home? When did this happen?"

"About the time you started texting me."

"Why?"

"Detective Stewart showed up at the shop again."

Faye sighed. "And he's worried about her finding out about—"

"Yes." His tone came out sharper than he intended. "Sorry. I'm going to be" — he made air quotes — "'working on the website' while I work to get her off my tail. Again."

Faye frowned and leaned back. "You think you can manage your mom while dealing with all of that?"

"I'm going to have to. It isn't like we have anyone else to ask."

"We could figure out something if we needed to. In fact, if I had a salon at home I'd be able to help with her between clients."

Brad nodded, not wanting to get into an argument. "But that's neither here nor there since we don't have anything set up. I'm going to have figure out a way to do my job at home and find Allison's killer while watching her."

"We can look into one of those adult daycares. I've seen signs around the neighborhood."

"Maybe. But she can't be that bad. She's been living on her own just fine until now. Surely, she doesn't need *that* much assistance."

Faye frowned. "She managed to break her arm getting her mail. I'm worried she's deteriorating fast."

"She probably tripped over something. I'll bet some kid

left a ball in her path and she didn't see it. Kids are always leaving crap like that on our sidewalks."

"The doctor said there wasn't anything to trip her. The neighbors who saw her fall say she just fell."

"It has to be something they haven't looked at. Her knee could've given out or maybe her back is giving her problems. She's the last person to complain about anything. I'm sure it has to be an issue that she let go too long. We'll get to the bottom of this while she's staying with us. Then when she gets the medical attention she needs — something beyond the emergency room — she'll be back to living at her own home."

Faye squeezed his hand. "Hopefully, they'll let us see her soon and she can give us her side. I'll let the nurse know we can take her in."

Brad thanked her and rubbed his temples. It was all too much. First his layoff — that's what it felt like. He couldn't go into work and he was stuck home.

How was he supposed to find a killer? That wasn't his job. *He* was a killer. Sure, he might be able to spot the signs, but he also might not. It depended on who was trying to frame him. If anyone actually was.

Rose was in jail for murdering Duke, and he hadn't guessed her at all. She'd been helping him try to find the killer.

What a joke. She was probably laughing at him the entire time.

Who was laughing now?

Since she had killed Duke — as far as he knew — she couldn't have killed Allison. That much was certain. She was behind bars. Either the wrong person was arrested or someone wasn't framing him. But given how everyone kept looking at him for the murders, it seemed unlikely that he wasn't being framed. What were the chances two people he openly didn't care for were killed?

Astronomically low.

That meant it was either someone from the neighborhood or someone from work. If the killer was somebody within the agency, it would be much more challenging to figure out. They were all pros. But he also knew their protocols, knew the way they thought. He might actually have the advantage. And if it was someone from the neighborhood, he had to figure out who hated him enough to pull this off. That seemed like an unlikely scenario.

Not impossible, but unlikely. Especially to frame Rose for the murder. She was a trained assassin and went along with the arrest charges.

He'd been attacked during his kill the same night Duke died.

It had to be someone from his company.

A chill ran down his back.

Someone he trusted was out to get him. Wanted to take him down either by killing him or getting him arrested.

Was Rose involved, or simply a tool? He thought back her to turning on him right before her arrest. Not only had she kidnapped Luna, but she'd expressed her disdain for him in no uncertain terms.

Had she meant what she'd said? Or had it been part of a greater plan to take him down?

But if that were the case, why would she take the fall? Maybe she really did hate him that much. Enough to risk life in prison.

Faye returned. "We can see her now."

Brad's stomach knotted. His mom had always been such a strong woman. Seeing her in the hospital with a broken arm and possibly a declined mental state made him shudder.

Faye helped him up. "They say she's in good spirits."

But would she remember him?

They walked hand-in-hand to the nurse's desk, then followed a doctor whose name Brad didn't catch. She rattled off a bunch of facts about dementia that Brad could easily look up later when his mind wasn't racing.

They entered the room.

Brad's breath hitched. He nearly didn't look at the bed, but made himself.

His mom had a cast on her arm and a few scratches on her face, but otherwise looked completely normal. Not frail, not weak, not out of her mind.

She even smiled as Brad neared. "Brad."

He stumbled as he took his last step to the bed. Forced a smile. "Mom, you gave us quite the scare."

She took his hand. Her skin was cool and smooth. "I gave myself quite the scare."

"How'd you fall?" He studied her, not sure what he was looking for.

"That's what I've been trying to remember. I was going to get the mail and then all of a sudden, I was on the ground and my arm hurt like the dickens."

"Did you trip over a child's toy? Maybe some kid left a ball out?"

"Maybe. I didn't see anything." She scrunched her face, looking deep in thought.

"Did your knee give out? You had problems with that before."

"When you were a teenager."

"What about your back? Ever since you had that rear-end collision, your lower back—"

"That only bothers me when it rains. And it was clear and sunny this afternoon."

Brad squeezed her hand. "Whatever happened, I'm

40

just glad it wasn't worse. How do you feel about staying with us for a while so you can recover?"

Faye appeared at his side. "We'll spoil you just like you do for us. I'll make your favorite dinner tonight."

His mom smiled. "I'd love that, but I don't want to put you out."

"Never. What else is family for? And the kids will be thrilled to see you."

Mom's smile faded. "Wait. What about Bingo?"

Brad held back a groan. He hadn't thought about his mom's Lhasa Apso that she'd let Luna name. "I can pick him up along with whatever else you need. Make me a list."

"Are you sure? I don't want to put you out."

"Mom, stop worrying about us. You're the one with a broken arm, and we have plenty of room. The guest room is all yours." He found a pad of paper with the hospital logo across the top in a drawer and handed it to her along with one of his pens from his coat. "Write out everything you need and I'll get it. No fussing."

She chuckled and began writing. Luckily, she had broken her left arm and could still use her right.

Brad spoke with Faye but paid more attention to what his mom wrote. Her writing was more loopy than normal, but was still perfectly readable.

How could the doctor think she had early-onset dementia? Aside from falling for no apparent reason, she seemed sharp as ever. She recognized him and Faye, knew her dog's name, and even remembered details about Brad's teenage years.

His mom was fine. In fact, she'd probably demand to return home within a matter of days.

She handed him the list. "This should be everything. Are you sure you don't mind? I can get all of that."

Faye put her hand on Mom's. "Nonsense. You need to rest. I'll drive you to our house and get you settled in while Brad picks up your things."

"Don't forget Bingo." She gave him a wide-eyed look.

"I wouldn't think of it." He kissed her cheek. "I'm going to speak with the doctor about when we can get you out of here."

He went out into the hall and looked around for the doctor, finding her leaving another room down the corridor.

She smiled at him. "Mr. Morris, do you have a question?"

"Yes, actually. Why do you think she has dementia? After speaking with her, she appears perfectly normal to me."

"Before you arrived, she said a few concerning things. Also, her neighbors were worried about her after she fell."

"Of course they were concerned. She broke her arm doing a simple task."

"She was asking for a neighbor who had died a few years back."

Brad shrugged. "So? She was a little confused. That could happen to anyone."

"These signs may not seem like much to you, but they're warnings we can't ignore."

"Sure. I appreciate you taking the time to let me know." He would get second and third opinions as soon as he got his mom discharged. "One more thing. She wrote this list. Nearly perfect penmanship and nothing forgotten."

The doctor took the paper and glanced at it. "I agree with you, but that doesn't change the fact that we're concerned about her. Like I told your wife, we suspect her to be in the early stages."

"I assume you'll offer us some resources."

"Yes. Those will be in the paperwork you receive upon her release."

"Perfect. Thank you." He headed back to the room and stopped cold when a thought struck him.

What if his mother's fall hadn't been an accident? That would explain her confusion and why she seems perfectly fine now.

Was the person going after him now trying to get to him through his family?

Anger burned. If that were the case, he would hunt down him or her and kill them himself.

They'd made a grave mistake messing with his family. He was now twice as determined to find them.

43

Chapter Six

BRAD SLAMMED his car door and looked up and down the sidewalk. Nothing littered the path, not even stray pebbles. If it had been this clear while his mom checked the mail, he couldn't imagine how she managed to break her arm.

Unless someone had cleared the path between then and now. He looked across the street, though it was hard to see much given the setting sun and the cloud cover. It may have been clear when she came out, but it would rain soon.

He marched across the street and scanned the sidewalk. It had more pebbles and even a plastic shovel in front of one house.

Maybe there *had* been something in Mom's way as she checked her mail. Her side of the road was a little too clear.

Brad snapped some pictures, then went back across the street and took more there. Then he checked her mailbox — it had a stack of envelopes. Obviously she hadn't made it that far before her mysterious fall.

He tucked those under his arm and went up her

walkway — also clear of anything to trip over — and unlocked the front door.

Bingo barked right away and circled Brad's feet. He reached down and patted the black-and-white mop of a dog. The dog licked his hand and whined. Probably had to relieve himself. Brad let him out back before looking over his mom's list.

Most of what she wanted would either be in her bedroom or bathroom. All basic stuff, plus he needed Bingo and some of his things.

Brad collected everything until the dog started barking. He let him in and prepared to take everything out to his car in trips when he passed his dad's old office. It looked as it did when he was alive, dusted and tidy. His mom obviously had the wherewithal to keep it up just as he'd left it.

As if he would come home any day.

He paused in the doorway, himself half-expecting his dad to hurry past him and tell him not to go in there. Funny how he could feel that way after so many years — almost thirty. Next year would be three decades since his passing. His murder.

The unsolved mystery of Brad's life, and also the reason he'd gotten into the assassination business in the first place. If he couldn't find his dad's killer, he could at least take out people like that devious bastard. And it did help. But it didn't completely scratch the itch.

Brad crept into the office, feeling like the sneaky teenager he'd been in years past going in there to feel a little closer to his old man. Though now he realized just how young his dad had been.

About Brad's current age.

Too young to die. Too young to leave his family.

He sat in the chair that still swiveled as well as it once

had and looked around the office, imagining his dad's perspective. What had he been doing before dying? Had he suspected anything?

Brad opened a few drawers and rifled through some papers on top of the desk. Nothing out of the ordinary. Just the home office of a family man.

Nothing like the secrets Brad's office held.

He really needed to find the murderer. If not for himself, for his mom. She deserved to have answers before her passing. Who knew when that would be? Given today's scare, it could be sooner rather than later. He hated thinking that, but it was reality.

None of them were getting any younger.

One more thing to add to his never-ending list of things to do. Figure out who was framing him. Take care of his mom. Solve an almost thirty-year-old murder. Help his teenagers deal with the death of their next door neighbor. Research and take out his next target.

What would he do if one more thing piled onto his list?

Brad closed his eyes, took a deep breath, and counted to thirty. There was no time to worry about what-ifs. The problems he already had were more than enough.

He started to leave, but stopped cold when he caught sight of a picture of himself with his parents. He had to have been sixteen. It would've been right before his dad's death.

It was definitely the last photo they had taken together.

Brad stumbled back and leaned against the desk, then felt his way over to the chair and collapsed onto it. Images from three decades earlier swirled through his mind, pulling him from the moment. He gasped for air, swearing his dad was in front of him.

The three of them were in the living room discussing

an upcoming family vacation — one that never happened. They were all so excited. Brad had wanted to invite Faye to come along. His parents argued that wouldn't be appropriate. Brad had insisted it would be fine, that he'd sleep on the floor if it would make them feel better. He just wanted to give her a break from dealing with her family.

To his parents' credit, they felt for her. Offered to help in other ways, but they didn't think bringing her on vacation was a good idea.

Then he and his dad were in his room, having a talk about the future. It felt too heavy for Brad, who thought they all had a lifetime ahead of them. But the way his dad spoke, it was like he knew his time was coming.

How could he know? A murder wasn't something he could've seen coming. Maybe he sensed his end was near? Or maybe he just wanted to get his son to focus on his schoolwork. Brad got good grades, but it had come fairly easy for him. Whenever he put in just a little more effort, he was usually able to get nearly perfect marks.

Brad drew in a deep breath and pulled himself from the spinning memories. Those were all in the past, and he needed to get back home. His mom would want her things and Faye would want his help settling her in.

He looked around the office one more time before rising. Despite his previous efforts, he had never come close to finding any clues. But now he knew so much more. Plus, technology had advanced by leaps and bounds. It seemed like new cold cases were solved every day.

It was time to focus back on his dad's case. Find an officer who would be willing to re-open the files and look for clues that were missed by officers in years past. Perhaps some DNA had been saved somewhere.

His gaze landed on a framed picture of his parents on

the desk. "I'm going to bring your killer to justice, and I'm going to do it before Mom passes away or loses her memories."

He didn't know how he would do it with everything else going on, but he would find a way.

Chapter Seven

"Bingo!" Luna pulled away from Faye and ran from the living room, calling out to her grandma's dog, who barked in return.

The shrill noise made Faye shudder. She really wasn't a dog person, but would have to get over that until Dianne was able to stay at her own home.

If she was able to. The doctor had seemed certain she was on the path to dementia. But Faye had driven her home and helped her into the house, and aside from being achy, her mother-in-law seemed just fine. On the way home, she'd smiled and joked. She'd even asked about each of the grandkids by name, remembering that Hadley loved acting, that Zeke was into video games, and that Luna had a ragdoll cat. And it was a good thing she'd remembered Mittens because otherwise Faye might've forgotten to lock her in Luna's room before Bingo arrived.

Faye was about to head to the entryway to see if Brad needed help bringing anything in when Dianne came over from the living room. Faye hurried over to her. "You don't have to get up. I'll help Brad take your things up to the guest room."

"I need to stretch my legs anyway. It doesn't take much for the blood to stop flowing these days." She rubbed her leg with her good arm to prove her point.

"If you're sure. Can I get you anything?"

"I'm fine. Might need some of that medication after dinner." She poked at her cast. "I don't know why they gave me a hard cast. Last time a soft one was plenty good."

"There's also a huge difference between a break and a hairline fracture. You—"

Bingo ran in and leaped on Dianne's leg. Luckily, she was a small dog, but Faye still reached out to help steady her mother-in-law.

"Oh, I missed you." Dianne patted the black-and-white pup who licked her hand incessantly.

"Zeke!" Faye called.

Her son appeared at the top of the stairs. "Yeah, Mom?"

"What are you doing up there?" Faye narrowed her eyes at him. "You're supposed to be watching Grandma in the living room."

"*She* told me to play my games — said she didn't want to be any trouble."

"And *I* told you to keep an eye on her."

He frowned. "Sorry."

"Never mind. Help your dad bring up her things to the guest room."

"Okay." He trudged down, grabbed the two smaller bags, then raced back upstairs.

Faye hurried over to Brad. "How'd everything go?"

"Getting her stuff? Fine."

She lowered her voice. "You didn't see any signs of dementia while she was there?"

He shook his head. "Everything looked as I'd expect. Even her list of needed items was exactly what anyone would ask for. The only thing that seems remotely strange is her breaking an arm while getting the mail."

"Did you see anything that would've tripped her? A crack in the sidewalk or anything?"

"Nothing. It was almost too perfect, if you know what I mean."

She nodded. "Like someone cleared away something she might've tripped over."

"Precisely. There was a ball across the street, proving that kids leave things lying around."

"Just like we thought. I'd really like to talk to that doctor again."

Brad picked up the rest of Dianne's bags. "Forget her. We need to set up a second and possibly even third opinion. That ER doctor is probably used to seeing the worst of the worst and is basing her assessment on that, not what's really going on."

"Maybe. I'll call our family doctor and see if he can get her in tomorrow or the next day."

"Let me. I'm going to be here all day."

"If you insist." She grabbed the dog food and bowls, and took them to the back door. On her way back to the entry, Luna nearly knocked her over, running after the dog. "Take Bingo to the backyard. That would be a better place to run around. Don't need to break another of Grandma's bones."

"Come on, Bingo!" Luna patted her legs and raced for the back door, laughing.

Faye looked at the last of Dianne's things but didn't have the energy to help bring them upstairs. She called for Zeke's help again before heading to the kitchen to figure out dinner. Originally, the plan had been leftovers, but there wouldn't be enough for an extra person. With any luck, the ground bison had thawed and she could make spaghetti and garlic bread. That usually fed an army, especially if she made extra veggies.

While she was checking on the meat — if she put it in warm water for a few minutes, it would be perfect — the doorbell rang.

Faye glanced out the window to see who it was but couldn't get a view of the front porch from her angle. With any luck, it wasn't the detective. They had enough to deal with without needing to answer additional questions about Allison's murder. Not to mention that Faye didn't want to think about her friend's death.

It was hard enough getting through the day without getting upset; she didn't need to add to her grief at home. She'd actually gotten her mind completely off the tragedy until now.

After setting the package of bison in a bowl of warm water, she crept toward the door to listen.

Brad was speaking to someone, but it wasn't the detective. It was a guy.

Relief washed through her. She tucked some loose hair behind her ear and made her way down the hall.

Wes and his kids stood at the door.

Her heart plummeted. So much for not thinking about Allison the rest of the night. She stepped next to Brad and slid her hand through his. "Can we help you, Wes?"

His face reddened. "I cannot believe you all had the nerve to show up at the funeral!"

The two younger kids looked away and Nate gave her and Brad an apologetic look.

Faye forced a smile. "She was my friend."

"Was she?" Wes's brows furrowed.

"Yes. She was over here almost every day. What has you so upset?"

"How can you even ask that?" He stepped toward Brad. "You know what everyone is saying."

"That Madonna should've taken the Oscar for best—"

"About my wife's murder!" Spittle flew from Wes's mouth. "Everyone agrees you did it!"

Brad's grip tightened around Faye's hand. "I was right here in this house the entire time. Do you remember? We even spoke."

"You can't prove that you didn't leave!"

Faye stepped closer to him. "Actually, he was talking to Larry the entire time Allison was gone. Larry even told that to the detective."

"Liars! Every one of you!"

Faye started to say something, but Brad pulled his hand away from her and pointed outside. "Let's take this outside if you're going to insist on doing this here. I can't believe you'd bring your children here for this spectacle."

Wes didn't back up. "Because I have nothing to hide. Can you say that much?"

"Of course I can! I didn't kill your wife. I'm sorry for your loss, but showing up at my house to blame me for the death isn't going to get you anywhere. I don't want to have to call the cops, but it's getting to the point where you aren't giving me any other choice."

Faye glanced around to make sure Luna hadn't joined them.

It appeared she and the dog were still in the backyard, but Zeke and Hadley were both nearby. Zeke was watching Brad and Wes with wide eyes and pulling on his hair. Hadley was exchanging horrified looks with Nate.

Faye stepped between her husband and Wes. "The kids

don't need to be here for this. If you'd like to talk with us, let's set up a time—"

"We're discussing this now! There isn't any reason for any of the kids not to be here. Unless someone is hiding the truth!"

"What about you?" Brad demanded. "Were *you* here at the time of the murder?"

"How dare you!" Wes swung for Brad.

He darted out of the way, pulling Faye with him. "I saw you after. Right before those millennials came back saying they'd found Allison. But I can't recall seeing you for a while before that. Everything was unusually quiet for a while. If you ask me, *that* is suspicious."

"I was here the entire time!" He lunged for Brad, who held out his palm and blocked the hit.

"I'm going to say this one time only." Brad stepped closer. "You need to leave. I refuse to discuss this any further in front of the kids. If you really think we have to talk about this, we can set up a time. And if you try to assault me one more time, I will press charges. Understood?"

"You think the cops wouldn't side with me? This is the second murder you're a suspect for."

Brad stepped so close to Wes that their noses nearly touched.

Faye moved in front of Hadley and Zeke in case things turned violent.

"I'm not a suspect in your wife's death." Brad's voice was eerily calm. "And Rose is in jail for Duke's death. Have you forgotten that?"

Wes laughed cruelly. "You think you aren't a suspect in my wife's death? You're the number one suspect!"

Brad poked Wes's shoulder. "Stop deflecting. We all know who is usually guilty in these cases — the husband!

And what's up with Allison's fake pregnancy? Seems like you have a lot to hide! What is it?"

Wes's face reddened. "How *dare* you accuse me in front of my children!"

"You mean like you're doing to me right now?" Brad exclaimed. "Get out of my house! If you so much as stumble and touch my lawn, I'm filing a restraining order. You have no idea who you're dealing with."

"And you don't know who you're messing with. You haven't heard the last from me."

Brad snorted. "Believe me, you haven't, either."

Faye drew in a deep breath and turned to her children.

They were both staring at their dad in shock.

"How dare he?" Brad slammed the door and turned to the kids. "You two need to stay away from that entire family. Wes is a lunatic, and I don't want you getting involved."

Hadley ran upstairs.

Zeke didn't budge.

Faye put her hand on Brad's arm. "Why don't you get a shower and relax? I'll get dinner going."

His nostrils flared. "That man has had it out for us since before Allison died. I need to find out why — what's one more thing to my already full list?"

"Try not to think about him. He's lashing out because he's angry and helpless. Everyone is questioning Allison's fake pregnancy, and he hasn't given anyone a good reason that I've heard. I'm sure he'll cool down given enough time."

"Or he'll just get worse. My bet is on that option." He stormed up the stairs.

Faye collected herself before heading into the kitchen.

If only she knew why her friend had been faking her pregnancy.

Chapter Eight

BRAD PUSHED his food around the plate, unable to stop thinking about Wes. Normally, he loved Faye's spaghetti, but tonight he couldn't taste anything. And his stomach was so tightly knotted, he couldn't even force himself to eat to avoid offending Faye.

"Brad?" Faye said.

He pulled himself from his thoughts and turned to her. "The food is delicious."

"Have you even had a bite? But that isn't what I asked you. Are you okay?"

"Yeah, of course. Great."

Everyone else's expressions told him they knew he was lying. Even Luna's.

He grimaced. "Okay, I'm not great. That much is clearly obvious. But I'll be fine. Wes will leave us alone, and we don't have to worry about him anymore. I just need to clear my head." He turned to his mom. "How are you doing? Sorry you came at a time when there's so much drama."

"Don't worry about me, son — unless you think I can help. Would you like me to talk with that young man?"

"Wes?" Brad scoffed. "No. I don't want you engaging him if you see him. He's dangerous."

"He's hurting."

"Doesn't mean he isn't dangerous." Brad looked around the table. "I don't want any of you talking to him."

"Never do, anyway," Hadley mumbled.

Brad glanced at her plate. She'd eaten even less than him. "You aren't on another one of your diets, are you?"

She scowled at him. "No."

"Then why haven't you eaten anything?"

"Why haven't *you* had anything?"

He clenched his jaw. "I'm the one asking questions."

"I'm not hungry." Hadley dropped her fork on her plate and with her eyes dared him to make a big deal about it.

"You need to eat or you'll waste away."

"Oh my gosh. I'm not going to waste away. If anything, I could stand to lose a few pounds."

"I knew it!" He threw down his napkin. "You're on a diet."

"No, I'm *not*."

"Then why aren't you eating?"

"Because I'm not hungry!"

"Eat your mom's food," he bellowed. "She spent a lot of time making a nice meal for us all!"

"*You* eat it." She stared him down.

Faye put a hand on his arm. "It's fine. We're all balls of nerves tonight."

"Not me." Luna grinned and shoveled in more spaghetti. "I can't wait for Mittens to meet Bingo."

"That's a bad idea," Zeke said. "Dogs and cats hate each other."

"Not Bingo and Mittens." She stuck her tongue out at him.

Brad pressed his palms on the table. "The cat and dog are not meeting. End of discussion."

"Boo." Luna pouted.

He turned his attention back to Hadley. "You need to eat. I know things have been tough on you, but you have to get nourishment."

She sighed over-dramatically. "I had a snack after school. Ate a ton of fries. If you saw how much I ate, you'd have told me to slow down."

"So, you filled up on garbage and now aren't eating your mother's cooking?"

"You're such a hypocrite!" She pushed her chair back and grabbed her plate. "I'm done."

Brad started to speak but his mom turned to Hadley. "Everyone is stressed out tonight. Don't feel bad. I know your dad didn't mean to upset you."

Hadley glared at Brad.

"I'll tell you what. Let me make you something else. Are you avoiding carbs, sweetheart?"

"Mother!" Brad rose, nearly knocking his chair over.

"No, Grandma." Hadley shook her head. "Really, I'm not hungry. I ate a bunch of food after school. Not only fries, but a double bacon cheeseburger."

"Definitely not on a diet," Zeke said.

She shoved him.

"Hey, I'm just trying to help."

"Don't." Hadley turned to her grandma. "Thanks for the offer, but I'm really just full. Next time I won't eat so much after school. I just wanted to celebrate."

"Celebrate what, honey?"

Hadley grinned. "I got the lead role in the new school play!"

The tension in the air melted away as everyone congratulated her. Everyone other than her brother. He frowned and pushed his own food around the plate.

Guilt stung, and Dr. Trellis's words ran through his mind. Brad patted Zeke's back. "You won first place in that competition on HardCorps the other weekend. That's something to be proud of."

"Not that any of you care about video games."

"Hey, I do. We all know how hard you try."

Zeke rolled his eyes.

"I'm serious."

"Whatever, Dad."

Brad sat back down. No matter what he did, nobody appreciated it. He may as well lock himself in his office and forget everything else, and research his next target. At least assassinating people was something he was good at. Even when he got jumped by two thugs, he'd been able to get away from them and take out his last hit.

Hadley marched toward the hall. "I'm going to my room."

"What are you doing tonight?" Faye asked.

"I just told you — going to my room."

"You aren't going out on a Friday night? Just going to hole up in your room?"

"Yeah. Is something wrong with that?"

Faye frowned. "It isn't like you. Are you sure everything is okay?"

Hadley's face reddened and she put her hands on her hips. "You guys, more than anyone, know that everything is *not* all right!"

"It would help to spend some time with your friends. What about Ellie? I haven't seen her in a while."

"I just want to be alone. That's it!" She stormed out of the room.

Faye started to go after her, but Brad stopped her. "Let her have some space."

"It isn't good for her to lock herself away from the world."

"Maybe it *is*. Not forever, but for now."

"How can being alone be good? What if her thoughts spiral?" Faye's eyes widened. "Do you know how many kids commit suicide these days? She could get online and some jerk could tell her to kill herself — and she might! I'm going up there."

Brad blocked her again. "I know you're worried, but she's a smart kid. She just needs to be alone with her thoughts to work through them. Dealing with this kind of loss isn't going away overnight."

"I'm going to take her phone so she can't get on social media."

Brad shook his head. "That'll just make her even more mad. She said she wants space, let's give it to her."

Faye pulled out her phone. "I'm calling Ellie."

"Don't you think Hadley would've called her friend if she wanted to?"

"She doesn't know what's good for her. I do! I'm her mother. She—"

"Whoa!" His mom stumbled, her good arm flying out. Her head was aiming for the table's corner.

Brad rushed over and caught her just before she made contact. "Are you okay?"

She regained her balance. "I don't know what just happened."

"Did you trip?"

"I'm not sure."

"What do you mean?"

His mom looked around. "There isn't anything on the ground. I couldn't have tripped."

"Over your own feet?"

"I haven't forgotten how to walk." She shook her head.

"Did your knee go out? Or—"

"I'm probably just tired. I should get upstairs and into bed. Are all my things in the guest room?"

Brad nodded to Zeke. "Help your grandma up the stairs." He turned back to her. "Everything from your list is upstairs, except for Bingo's things. I'll set him up by the back door."

"Nonsense. He always sleeps on my bed."

"Okay, then. While Zeke helps you upstairs, I'm going to make sure Bingo does his business outside before taking him up to your room."

Faye followed him while he took the dog to the back-yard. "I'm really worried about Hadley."

Brad rubbed his temples. "I'm worried about everyone."

"What if she kills herself? I just read about a girl her age who was getting bullied online and she took her own life. Her parents had no idea what was going on. They're completely devastated now."

He put his arms around her and rested his chin on her shoulder. "Hadley isn't getting bullied. Everyone adores her. Not only is she talented and popular, but she's nice to everyone."

"And she usually goes out every weekend. Now she isn't. Something is definitely wrong, and it's more than Duke's passing."

Brad drew a deep breath and watched the little dog prance around the yard, smelling every blade of grass. "Her boyfriend was murdered and she hasn't told anyone other than us. She needs time to process it. Remember when my dad was killed? I was a wreck for a long time."

"But there's a difference between losing a parent and a guy she hadn't been seeing for very long."

"We don't know how serious their relationship was. All we know is that she was in love, and you know how overwhelming those feelings are at that age. If anything would've happened to you, it would have ruined my life."

"Now it sounds like you approve of their relationship."

"It doesn't matter what I think about it. The fact is, our daughter is dealing with a major loss. If she needs some alone time, it isn't alarming."

"You have to agree that going out with her friends would be good for her."

"Then call Ellie, but Hadley could still say no. And we're going to have to be okay with that. She's seventeen. Let her figure out how to deal with this her own way."

Faye sighed. "It isn't healthy to be alone."

"You keep saying that, but some people find solitude comforting."

She pulled away. "I'm going inside to call Ellie."

"Let me know how that goes." Brad whistled for the dog's attention. He still hadn't done anything other than sniff the entire yard.

Once Bingo finally relieved himself, Brad led him up to the guest room.

His mom was arranging some of her things on top of the dresser. She patted the bed, and Bingo leaped up and curled into a ball. "Thanks for taking him out."

"I'm happy to do whatever you need."

"I could use some help getting out of this shirt."

"I'll find Faye." He made his way to the door and paused. "You really don't remember what happened downstairs? When you started to fall?"

"No. I just remember the table was coming at me quickly." She frowned.

"Is that what happened when you fell near the mailbox?"

"I'm not sure. The whole thing is foggy. I remember walking toward the mailboxes and the next thing I knew, I was on the ground in pain." She rested her hand on the cast.

"Would getting a cane help?"

"Now you think I'm getting old."

"It has nothing to do with that." He gave her a reassuring glance. "But you fell once and nearly did another time — all in one day. Has this happened before?"

"I don't think so."

"You don't *think* so, or you haven't?"

She pinched her nose. "All I know is that I'm tired. I want to climb into bed and catch up on the news."

"Before going to sleep?"

"Yes. I like to know what's going on in the world."

"That stuff will give you nightmares. I'll get Faye to help you with your pajamas." He headed back into the hall and found his wife in their bedroom, finishing up a phone call.

She tossed the phone on the bed. "I've spoken with several of Hadley's friends. They all say she's busy with homework all weekend."

"Then give her space."

"I'll never forgive myself if she takes her life! I have to intervene. You aren't talking me out of this."

Brad sighed. "She's going to resent you."

"At least she'll be alive."

"Okay. I'll talk with her. Can you help my mom? She can't get her shirt off with that cast."

"Of course. You'll convince Hadley to get out?"

"Yes." He hated doing that to his daughter, but he also couldn't stand to see Faye so tightly wound.

"Thank you." She kissed him before leaving the room.

Brad took some ibuprofen before knocking on Hadley's door.

"Go away!"

"I just want to ask you something."

"I'm not going anywhere," she called.

He tried the knob. Locked. "Will you let me in?"

Silence.

"I'm not going away."

The door opened. "What do you want?"

"Your mom is really worried about you."

"I just want to be alone."

"And I get that, but she thinks getting out would do you good."

Hadley's brows drew together. "It won't."

"Would you consider going out for just a little while? Drive yourself so you can leave early."

Her mouth formed a straight line. "I've already told all my friends I'm not going anywhere. And by the way, do you know how humiliating it is that Mom called them? I could die of embarrassment."

"Don't tell her that."

"Huh?"

"Never mind. Would you just go out for a little while?"

She crossed her arms and shook her head so vehemently her hair whipped in her face.

"I understand how you feel. Really, I do. But would it hurt to get out and see your friends?"

"Yes. All I want is to listen to depressing music and look through photos."

They went back and forth until Faye joined them. "Are you getting together with Ellie?"

"I can't believe you called my friends!" She yanked the door toward her.

Faye grabbed it before Hadley could close it. "If you won't go out with your friends, take Zeke somewhere."

"Zeke?" Hadley looked at her like she'd lost her mind.

"Yes. There are bunch of new movies this weekend. Go to the theater and watch one."

"You're crazy."

"Nope. I'm thinking straight. And I'll pay. Get out of your pajamas, and I'll get some cash from my purse." She walked away.

"I'll go to that party with Ellie! The one with all that beer."

Faye shook her head without turning around.

Hadley threw Brad a pleading look.

He held up his hands. "Her mind is made up."

"Ugh!" Hadley slammed the door.

Brad went to his son's room to break the news to him.

Chapter Nine

HADLEY HANDED ZEKE HIS POPCORN. "Let's get to our seats before anyone I know sees us."

"You think I'm happy about this?"

"Never said you were. But you could've worn something that didn't go out of style thirty years ago." She glared at his orange vest.

"It was the only thing that was clean. And besides, this style is coming back."

"Like you'd know." She looked at the ticket. "Awesome. We have to go all the way to the back of the building. Someone is definitely going to see us together."

"I'd rather be at home. HardCorps is having a huge event this weekend. I could be earning points as we speak."

Hadley faked a yawn. "Let's just make the best of this. At least we found a movie we both want to see."

They hurried to the theater, making it most of the way down the long hall without running into anyone from school.

Until a group of middle school girls from the neighborhood rounded a corner. One of the girls snickered and pointed at Zeke. "You trying out for *Back to the Future* or something?"

His expression tightened. "You wish."

Hadley held back an eyeroll and stepped closer to the little brat. "Leave him alone."

"Why should I?" She flipped her hair behind her shoulder and smirked.

"Because he's smarter and funnier than you'll ever be."

One of the other girls snorted. "As if."

"Not only that, but he's more secure." Hadley sized her up. "You copied your outfit from the cover of *last* month's *Super Style* magazine."

The girl's mouth fell open.

"At least Zeke isn't afraid to be himself. He'll remember this when he's a millionaire and you're waitressing at some greasy diner." Hadley grabbed his arm and pulled him away, ducking into their theater. "That's what you get for being so obsessed with the 80s. You have to decide if you want people to like you or if you want to be seen as a freak."

"Seen as?" He lifted a brow, the corners of his mouth twitching. "You don't think I *am* one?"

"Ugh. Come on."

They found some seats near the back and off to the side, where hopefully nobody she knew would see them if they came in.

Hadley sipped her pop. "Hand me the licorice."

"I don't have it." Zeke slurped his drink.

She double-checked her lap. "Well, I don't."

He shrugged. "That stuff is gross, anyway."

"You'd know gross." She put her popcorn and the other candy on the tiny tray. "I'm going back to get the licorice. Do you need anything while I'm up?"

"Seconds on popcorn." He handed her his empty bag.

"You downed that already?" she exclaimed.

"Yep."

Hadley shook her head in disbelief and made her way down the stairs, careful to avoid any sticky spots. She shouldn't have worn her new boots, cute as they were. One wrong step and she'd have to spend an hour wiping down the soles to get them back to their current shape.

After arguing with the kid behind the counter about the licorice she didn't receive, she almost forgot to have Zeke's popcorn refilled. She loaded it with flavored salt — another of his gross preferences — and spun around.

Nearly knocked over some guy and barely avoided spilling the popcorn.

She swore, trying to catch it.

The dude spun around and helped her steady it.

Nate.

Her face flamed. "Thanks."

"Yeah, no problem. You okay?"

"I guess. My parents made me bring Zeke to the movies. Neither of us want to be here." Why was she spilling her guts to him? Just because they'd shared a greasy meal?

He didn't seem to notice, keeping his gaze on his hands. "Hey, I'm really sorry about my dad. He's been going crazy lately."

It took Hadley a moment to figure out what he was talking about. With everything else going on, she'd nearly forgotten about Wes showing up at their house to accuse her dad of murder. "He just wants to find the killer. My dad isn't the guy."

"I know." Nate sighed. "And I tried telling him that, but he wouldn't listen. Made all of us come over while he raged like a lunatic."

"The police figured out who killed Duke. I'm sure they'll do the same for your mom."

Their gazes locked, and she had a hard time pulling hers away.

Nate cleared his throat. "So, uh, what movie are you and your brother watching?"

"*Romancing the Zombie.* You?"

He shoved his ticket in his pocket. "Something lame. Mind if I join you?"

"Sure. Come on."

They went back to the theater, and luckily there was still a seat on the other side of Zeke — not that it was surprising.

"Move down," she told him. "Nate's joining us."

"I'm comfortable."

She glowered at him.

"Fine." He gathered his snacks and put them all on the tray next to him.

They barely had time to get settled when the lights dimmed. She hated to admit that it was just what she needed — that her mom had been right about getting out. No, she wasn't at the party with Ellie and Lucy and their other friends, but it wasn't so bad being with Nate and Zeke. She and Nate had actually laughed at all the same lines.

Once in the parking lot, Hadley started to say goodbye to Nate but he spoke first.

"Do you guys want to go to that ice cream place on Pike and Third? I heard they're having half-off banana splits tonight. Anniversary celebration or something."

Zeke's eyes widened. "Yeah. Let's go."

Hadley dug into her purse. She bumped her cell phone and when the screen lit up, it showed she had a ton of missed texts. "I have to see if we have enough money. Mom only gave us a fifty."

"Don't worry about it," Nate said. "It's on me."

"You sure?"

"It's the least I could do after what my dad pulled."

"Thanks," Zeke said. "But that wasn't your fault."

"I know. I still feel bad about that. He was totally out of line. Besides, I really don't feel like going home yet."

Hadley felt bad for him. She wouldn't want to go home to Wes, either.

Zeke turned to Hadley. "Can we go?"

"Yeah. I don't know how you have room for a banana split, though."

He grinned. "I always have room for ice cream."

"See you there in a few." Nate headed down the opposite way of the parking lot.

"He's cool," Zeke said. "Even though his dad is a jerk."

"I guess." Hadley marched toward her car and dug out her phone to see what she'd missed. Probably a group chat, given how many missed messages she had.

Nope. Just from Ellie. What was she freaking out about? Had something gone wrong at the party?

"I have texts, too." Zeke held out his phone. "My friends want to know why I'm not on HardCorps."

Hadley rolled her eyes as she scanned the messages. Lucy was asking about Nate, of all people. A few texts down explained why — apparently Lucy had seen Hadley eating with Nate after Hadley had put off getting together with her.

Now all their friends thought she and Nate had a secret fling.

As if.

Hadley tapped a message as quickly as she could, trying to put out the fire before word spread. That was the last thing she needed. Nate was the kind of guy she could really be good friends with, but something like this could scare him off. And he knew her secret.

Ellie responded almost as soon as Hadley sent her text. They went back and forth, with Ellie not believing that Hadley wasn't hiding a relationship with Nate and Hadley insisting on the truth.

Maybe she should've told her best friend about Duke. Then at least she would know why Hadley was so depressed lately. But she hadn't wanted to get Duke in trouble, so she'd kept their secret from everyone.

Nobody had guessed. Not even Ellie.

She was that good.

Or she had been. Ellie didn't believe her about Nate, and the more she tried to convince her, the less Ellie believed her.

"We gonna go anytime this century?" Zeke threw her an exasperated look.

"Be patient. You aren't going to die of starvation."

"Is that a jab about my weight?"

"It means this is important, so chill."

He crossed his arms. "You can text at the ice cream place, you know."

"Not until I deal with this." If anyone saw her at the theater with Nate, Ellie and Lucy would freak out. She'd never be able to convince them she wasn't seeing Nate.

"You shouldn't leave him waiting. He was nice enough to buy our banana splits."

Hadley glared at him. "You're so annoying!"

He shrugged.

She sent one more text, saying that Nate was Zeke's new best friend, and started her car.

"I'm not annoying."

"You need a dictionary. You'll find your picture as the

definition." Hadley pulled out of the spot and sped through the parking lot. Nate was probably already at the ice cream place.

"I don't know how you're so popular. Are you mean to everyone? Or just me?"

"I'm not mean to you." She pulled into traffic. "I'm honest."

"Is that what you tell yourself?"

"I'm not going to lie to you. And look around — even after Duke gave you advice on being cool, you still get picked on."

"You're just jealous."

"About what?" She sped through a yellow light.

"Do Mom and Dad know you drive like this?"

"We're late. I thought you wanted a banana split."

He sighed dramatically and turned the music to some 80s song.

"Seriously?" Hadley turned it back to the Top 20 song that had been playing. "You can pick the music when you drive."

Zeke mumbled something she couldn't make out.

"Why would I be jealous of you?"

"Because I was spending time with Duke. I saw the way you looked at him."

Heat flooded her face, her whole body. Her brother had noticed?

"See? You can't even deny it."

"I'm not, and have never been, jealous of you. End of discussion." She pulled into the parking lot of the ice cream place and drove around twice until she found a spot, her brother teasing her the entire time. She tried to block him out as she looked for a spot at the far end of the lot. Apparently everyone was going to the anniversary celebration for inexpensive desserts.

Before they reached the shop, she saw Nate was already inside.

"Sorry we're late," she said as they rushed over.

"She was too busy texting," Zeke said.

She glared at him before turning to Nate. "You know how it is with kids at school."

He gave her an easy smile. "Banana splits all around?"

They agreed and thanked him.

Five minutes later, the three of them were crowded around a little table meant for two.

"Looks like everyone had the same idea," Nate said.

Hadley's phone buzzed in her purse. Dread washed through her. Had someone seen her here with Nate and texted Ellie or Lucy? She looked around before digging out her phone.

"You couldn't go ten minutes without that thing." Zeke shook his head.

"Do you realize this isn't the 80s? People use cell phones. It how they stay connected. You should try it."

He glared at her, his face turning pink.

Hadley felt bad for embarrassing him but didn't apologize. She opened her texting conversation, her mind racing with excuses for why she was crammed next to Nate — any closer and she'd practically be on his lap thanks to the crowd.

But the text from her best friend wasn't an accusation.

Ellie: Noah saw u and Z with N. Guess you're right!

Hadley: Like I said.

She added some smiling emojis at the end to make sure she didn't sound bad. Now she was worried about how she sounded — her brother was getting in her head.

As she closed the texting conversation, a photo of her and Duke kissing appeared on the screen. She closed the screen.

Zeke's eyes widened.

Too late.

She played it cool. "What? Are you choking?"

"Was that a picture of you kissing Duke?"

"You're up way past your bedtime — you're seeing things."

He reached for her purse. "Let me see that."

Nate cleared his throat. "Hey, Zeke. They're handing out raffle tickets. Want to see what they're for? Maybe we can win something cool."

Zeke whipped his head around, his eyes wide. "Be right back."

Hadley's bones turned to rubber for a moment. "Thanks for the save."

"No problem. Glad I ran into you. Tonight has been a lot more fun with company."

"Even Zeke?"

"He isn't so bad."

She turned back to her melting banana split.

"Was that a picture of Duke?"

Hadley nodded.

"Don't worry. Your secret is safe with me."

Chapter Ten

BRAD KISSED Faye and Luna as they left for her soccer practice. Eighties music blared from upstairs, where Zeke didn't want to be disturbed as he tried to regain lost ground in the competition for his video game.

He returned to the kitchen, where his mom was hand-washing the dishes despite her broken arm. "You can just put those in the dishwasher."

"It always comes out better when they're done by a person." She gave him a sweet smile and turned back to the sink.

He wrapped the leftover pancakes in plastic and stuck them in the fridge. "You don't need to do that. Why don't you rest?"

"I need to keep busy. Don't want my mind or my body to start failing."

"At least let me do this." He took the plate from her hands. "You need to at least rest your broken arm."

"If you insist. Will you at least walk around the neighborhood with me?"

"Of course." He piled the remainder of the dishes and pans into the washer and turned it on. "How'd you sleep?"

"Almost as well as at home. It's nice to be so close to everyone."

"It's great to have you here."

"I hope I'm not in the way."

"Never." He helped her into her jacket and put Bingo's leash on.

She stepped onto the porch and took a deep breath. "Nothing like fresh morning air in the spring. I can smell the ocean."

Brad locked the door and looked around the yard. Though the sun was poking through the clouds, raindrops dripped from the trees and eaves from an overnight drizzle. "Can't beat Pine Harbor this time of year."

Bingo yipped and bounced around, tugging on the leash.

"Want me to take him?" Brad asked.

"Nonsense."

He helped her down the steps nonetheless. Birds chirped, and in the distance a rainbow decorated the sky above the trees.

Maybe today would be a good day.

They turned left and greeted a few neighbors. Some little kids stopped to pet Bingo, who eagerly licked them in return.

His mom turned to him. "Such lovely neighbors."

"They can be."

They turned at the first intersection toward a dog park. It wasn't too far, but he wasn't sure she could make it. But it was her arm that was broken, not her legs.

Just as they were about to turn again, Detective Stewart stepped out from an unmarked black sedan.

Brad's stomach turned. So much for it being a good day.

He pretended not to see her and kept going.

"Mr. Morris!"

"Detective Stewart." He held back a groan.

She held her hand out to his mom and they exchanged introductions.

"It was nice seeing you." Brad stepped away.

"Actually, if you don't mind, I have a few questions."

"I'm on a walk with my mother." He loved pointing out the obvious. "Perhaps we can talk when we return."

"This will only take a moment."

His mom turned to him. "Is everything okay, Bradley?"

He nodded. "There's been some, er, activity in the area. Nothing to worry yourself about. How about walking on ahead and I'll catch up in a moment."

"Sounds good." She turned to the detective. "My Brad is a good guy. He'll help you with whatever you need. He's just like his dad in that way. Such a hard worker, even working on weekends and evenings to take care of the family. Two jobs in one. He—"

"Mom." Brad cleared his throat. "The detective doesn't need to hear about all of this." He turned to Stewart. "Her medications are making her more talkative than usual. I apologize."

"It's not my medications." His mom frowned. "I'm proud of you and your dad. No two better men ever lived. All I'm doing is letting the officer know what a fine person you are. It'll help her investigation."

Detective Stewart smiled. "I appreciate that, Dianne. Enjoy your walk."

Brad watched as his mom strolled down the sidewalk. "What's so important?"

"Nothing new, really. I keep—"

"So, that means I can go? Great."

Stewart frowned. "No. As I've been looking into Allison's murder, your name keeps coming up. Just like it did with Duke Hill's."

"I was cleared of that, and this time I was with a whole group of people in my home. Most of the neighborhood saw me there. I didn't have anything to do with either of the crimes."

"Yet the consensus is, you didn't like either one of them."

"Is that a crime now?" He glanced at his mom to make sure she wasn't getting too far ahead.

"No, but it is concerning."

"My obvious innocence?"

The corners of her mouth curved up. "The coincidences."

He gave a bored sigh. "Meaning?"

"Both were killed with knives from your company. Duke was murdered by your colleague. You didn't like either of the deceased."

"I had no idea about Rose's involvement with my neighbor. Didn't know they had a relationship until you mentioned it."

The detective straightened her stance. "Were you involved in the plots to murder Duke Hill or Allison Campbell?"

He held her gaze. "No, I was not."

"How close are you to Rose Flores?"

"Haven't spoken with her since she kidnapped my daughter."

Stewart gave him a knowing look. "Were you close to her prior to that?"

"No."

"You worked with her. Trained her."

She'd obviously done her homework. But the question was, what did she think he had trained her in? She couldn't know about the assassin business, or Rose would be dead already.

"Yes," he said. "I trained her about BlueBlade knives, but she didn't make it easy. I was glad to be done and get back to my normal work."

"I've never seen you working in the store. What is it you do, exactly?"

The detective was getting dangerously close to things she couldn't know anything about.

Brad glanced at his mom again. "Currently, I'm working on the website. Needs updating."

"Sounds like you're a jack of all trades around there."

"I do what they ask."

She made a few notes on her phone. "And what about the party? Were you there the entire time?"

"For the five-hundredth time, yes."

"How did you learn about Allison's murder?"

"When that millennial came back and told us."

"Do you remember her name?"

"Not off the top of my head. Look, I need to catch up with my mother, who was hospitalized yesterday. If you really want to find real leads, question Wes about the fake pregnancy. He had to have known about that — and if not, they really had issues."

"I'm aware of the fake pregnancy."

He inched away. "Good. Are you aware Wes showed up at my house last night and nearly punched me? I moved out of the way, or I'd have a nice bruise to show you."

"He assaulted you?"

"Threw accusations at me in front of my family and then *tried* to hit me. Doesn't seem like a mourning widower to me. Sounds more like a man with something to hide, but

I'm no detective. Talk to you later." He hurried away, relieved to finally be free of her.

For now.

She wouldn't leave him alone for long. Wes would undoubtedly tell her something that would send her running to question him.

He needed to get home and get to work. Figuring out who was trying to frame him was his number one priority.

That person needed to go down. If not to prison, then by Brad's own hand.

It only took a minute to catch up to his mom. She had stopped to let some other kids pet Bingo.

Brad gave a friendly greeting to the kids' mom, who promptly ushered them back to their yard.

"You have such a friendly neighborhood." His mom smiled.

His only response was to loop his arm through hers.

"What did the detective want?"

"Just had a few questions about a case. No big deal." He calculated how long it would take to get to the dog park. "How are you holding up? There's a dog park about ten minutes away. We can go there or head back. It's up to you."

"I'm up for it. Bingo would love to run around with other dogs."

The rest of their walk was uneventful. The dog owners at the park didn't recognize him, and were nice. On the way back, he took his mom a different route to avoid the detective.

And it worked.

Once inside, his mom busied herself with a crossword puzzle and he went up to his office, leaving the door cracked so he could hear if she needed him — not that he would likely hear anything over Zeke's music.

He pulled up a list of all the current and recent Blue-Blade employees, organizing them based on how well they knew Rose. Brad was the only one who never spent time with her. The younger guys were practically her BFFs — as Hadley would say. But all of the guys spent time with her. It was easy to weed out the employees who knew nothing about the assassinations. Rose wouldn't be working with them.

That still left a lot of potential suspects. Though there were only a few who showed any real irritation with Brad. Given how high up he was in the company, most tried to stay on his good side.

He had to dig deeper. Who would have *reason* to want him out of the way? Rose was the only obvious answer. There were a few guys close to his rank, but they received as many cases as Brad so it wouldn't make any sense that they would want to go after him.

After an hour of going through the list of employees numerous times, he wasn't any closer than he'd been when he started.

Could that mean it was one of his neighbors? Rose *had* buddied up with more than a few of the husbands at the Super Bowl party. She'd been eating with some of them at the bar the night Brad showed up — the night Wes sent a picture of him with Rose to Allison, knowing she'd tell Faye.

The person out to get him could be anybody.

He needed some kind of lead.

Brad called Kurt to leave a message, and he nearly dropped the phone when his boss answered on the second ring.

"Hey, Brad. Is everything okay?"

Brad closed the office door and got right to the point

STACY CLAFLIN & NOLON KING

before Kurt ended the call. "You've spoken to Rose since her arrest, right?"

"A few times. She isn't going to say anything. We all know the consequences. The Felix incident."

A shudder ran down his spine. "Right. But that isn't my concern. Do you think she was working with someone?"

"At BlueBlade?"

Brad bit back a sarcastic reply. "Correct."

"We have no reason to believe she did. Why? Did you come across something?"

"No. I just—"

"You have a lot on your plate. I get it. The police are breathing down your neck and now your mom."

Brad jolted. Kurt shouldn't know anything about his mom. He hadn't found out about her injury until he was getting into his car.

Was his mom's injury more than an accident?

He fell onto his chair, his mind spinning out of control.

"Tell you what." Kurt's voice pulled Brad from his thoughts. "I just had my afternoon appointment cancel. Bring Faye here to my house at one and we can chat over lunch. Hopefully, I can put your mind at ease."

"Sure."

At least that would give him a little time to figure out exactly what he would ask Kurt. One visit might not be long enough to figure out even half of what he needed to know.

Chapter Eleven

FAYE RUSHED INTO THE CAR, a rolled-up paper sticking out of her purse, and slammed the door. "Sorry I'm late. I swear, Luna's coach just likes to hear herself talk. I couldn't get away any sooner."

"What's the paper for?" He waited for her to buckle in, then pulled out of the driveway.

She pulled it out. "I meant to leave that in the house. We can talk about it later."

"What is it?"

Faye sighed. "I don't want to distract you. Let's just focus on the lunch at Kurt's."

"Now I'm too curious. At least tell me."

She hesitated. "I drew up some plans for turning that spare room by the front entry into my home salon."

He groaned.

"I told you we should wait."

"We may as well talk about it now while we have some uninterrupted time."

"Are you sure?"

He turned onto the main road. "Yep."

"I figured out a way to keep people from the main house, knowing what a concern that is for you. We can make a separate entrance right next to the garage. It'll come in right at the corner of the room — of the salon — and I can lock the main doors during business hours or even take out the door altogether if we don't want to see the salon from the entry. A lot of this is flexible. And best of all, it allows more freedom to stay home with your mom."

"But how will that work if you're locked away from her?"

"She doesn't need someone watching her every moment."

"What if it comes down to that?"

Faye sighed. "I'm sure we can come up with something. If things get that bad, I'm sure she'll get a nurse coming in to check on her."

"For eight hours a day?"

"I didn't say it was a perfect plan. Obviously, we'll have to figure some things out together, but this is a starting point. Otherwise, I can't help with her at all. Not when I have to drive into the salon every day."

"Not that it's really an issue with me home now."

"What about when you have to go back into the shop? Or when you have to, uh, you know … do the other side of the business."

"You mean the assassinations. Those are pretty much always at night — when you're home."

From the corner of his eye, he watched her fidget.

"It isn't bad, remember? I'm removing dangerous people from society that the law can't touch. People like me are necessary to keep things running smoothly where the system fails. Which unfortunately it does a lot."

She sighed. "I know. It's hard to get used to."

"It wasn't easy for me to adjust to, either."

"I wish you'd have let me in. We could've gone through that together."

"That wasn't possible. We're not supposed to tell our families. That reminds me — don't say anything while we're over at Kurt's. You're going to have to pretend to not know anything. I only told you because there was no other way around it."

"You can trust me."

The GPS system alerted him that they were almost there — as if entering the gated neighborhood with huge houses wasn't clue enough.

He pulled into the driveway of the towering house with immaculate everything. Nothing was out of place, no blade of grass too long. It made him appreciate his neighborhood where things had character. Nobody noticed if someone's lawn got slightly unruly. It was a place where people lived, and it showed.

Brad waited for Faye to close her door before setting the alarm, though he doubted it was needed in a place like this. He took her hand and they strolled up the walkway. His nerves were on fire, knowing their every move was probably on camera — not just on a doorbell cam like where they lived.

Kurt opened the door before Brad even knocked. He nodded to Brad, then kissed Faye's hand. "So nice to have you two here again. It's been too long. Come in."

They followed him to the dining room where a girl not much older than Hadley, wearing a traditional French maid uniform, was setting out plates. She hurried away without a word.

Kurt talked about the latest sports team win as he helped Faye into her seat and called for the main course. "I hope nobody's allergic to roast lamb. I didn't think to ask when we were on the phone."

"It's fine." Brad scooted himself in between his wife and boss.

Kurt rambled on about a new knife in the works for the company, one that would become the face of BlueBlade. "People will forget about the Valderdorf once they see this one."

"That's great." Brad wanted to ask if Kurt's desire to make people forget about the famous curved blade was because of the attention it had been getting from Duke and Allison's murders.

As the young girl and a slightly older one filled the table with mouthwatering foods, Kurt's wife came into the room. She was just as polished as everything else.

"You remember MaryAnne?" Kurt asked.

Brad and Faye both said yes and greeted her.

Everyone made light conversation, laughing often, over the meal. As soon as the girls arrived to clear the table, MaryAnne ushered Faye away to show her their newest horse.

Kurt pulled some Cuban cigars from a drawer and handed one to Brad while the older server poured them both scotch. "What's your biggest concern?"

Brad sipped his drink and waited for the girls to leave before speaking.

"You can speak in front of them. They won't say anything." He puffed his cigar.

"Great." He held back a cringe, thinking of what would happen to them if they did.

"You think Rose was working with someone within our organization?" Kurt leaned back and studied Brad.

"I'm not sure what to think at this point, except that

the second murder was too much of a coincidence to actually be one."

Kurt nodded and waved his cigar for Brad to continue.

"She made friends with some of my neighbors — including Allison's husband. He sent a picture of Rose and me together outside of work, making sure Faye would see it."

"And you think they were working together to frame you for the murders? Did he want his wife dead?"

"I don't know them well enough to know the answer to that. He blames me, though."

"Was he at your party during the murder?"

Brad frowned. "It's too hard to say. The police don't have an exact time of death. You know how that goes."

Kurt nodded and poured himself more drink. "Want some?"

"No. Wes was definitely at the party, but I wasn't watching him. He could've easily snuck away — or he could've hired someone."

"But Rose was already arrested for your other neighbor's murder."

"Yes."

Kurt leaned forward. "Rose knows the consequences. She's eager to get herself out of the slammer. I've hired one of my best attorneys to work her case, so she has a shot. But either way, she's staying silent. None of us are at risk of her ratting us out. The woman doesn't want to suffer a slow, torturous death."

"She went rogue and you're giving her an attorney?"

"Truth be told, I don't care what any of you do during your own time. Kill who you want, but don't let it lead back to BlueBlade."

"But everything she did—"

"Don't worry about Rose. I've spoken with her several times."

"She tried to kill me!"

Kurt raked his hands through his hair. "And if she ever becomes a free woman, she'll be demoted. We always have consequences. Now, what is it you need from me? I'm a busy man, so we need to get to the point."

"How did you know about my mother's injury?"

"I always know what my employees are doing. Always."

Brad gave him a double-take. "So, you knew Rose killed Duke all along? Is that why you were avoiding me?"

"Listen, I don't blame you for being paranoid. You have a lot on your plate — that's why you have the time to work from home. Settle your affairs before coming back. Let me help you. But to do that, you have to tell me what you need from me."

"The two murders in my neighborhood are not a coincidence! Either Rose killed Duke, and is working with someone else who killed Allison, or she's innocent and somebody else is framing me."

"If she didn't do it, then my attorney will get her out. That isn't a question."

"Have you spoken with her?" Brad demanded.

"I've already told you, several times."

"Did she say whether she killed them?"

"Him," Kurt corrected. "And no. That wasn't my concern. I had to make sure she wasn't going to breathe a word about my business."

"That doesn't help me!"

"You can speak with Howard. He'll make sure you don't see the inside of a jail, if that's what you're worried about."

"Obviously, I want to avoid that. But what I'm most concerned with is finding out who's framing me."

Kurt leaned over and patted Brad's shoulder. "Tell you what. I'll dig around some more with the guys Rose was friends with at the shop. They aren't involved — I'd know if they were — but if it'll put your mind at ease, I'd be happy to press them for details."

"You'd do that?"

"Of course. I'll take it a step further and have anyone suspicious followed for a while. If anyone from BlueBlade is framing you, I'll ferret out the traitor. However, if I were you, I'd put them out of my mind now to save you time and energy. She was only friends with the young ones. They don't have enough experience to pull off something so complicated."

Brad breathed a sigh of relief. "That would help. Then I can focus on my neighbors. It just as easily could be one of them."

"Good, good." Kurt gave him a crooked smile before emptying his glass a second time. "You're not worried about any of the older assassins? I can look into them, too."

Brad frowned. Those were *his* friends. If they had a beef with him, they'd let him know to his face. They wouldn't be a weasel and frame him for multiple murders. "No, it wasn't any of them. Rose spoke with them even less than me."

"Makes sense. She's always been intimidated by you old-timers."

Brad arched a brow.

Kurt waved him off. "You know what I mean. Those of you who have been around longer, who have more experience. You all could snap the necks of the lower assassins in your sleep."

Yet Rose had gotten the better of Brad, could've killed

him, because she'd managed to kidnap his daughter and divert his attention.

Kurt looked at his watch. "We should do this again, but for now I need to get to my next appointment. I'll be in touch about anything I find in the shop. You'll let me know if you find anyone guilty in your neighborhood?"

"Yes."

"Don't kill them yourself. We don't want any trails leading to you and thus BlueBlade. I'll call my cousin who runs a similar operation on the East Coast."

"Sounds like a plan." Brad rose and shook Kurt's hand, studying him. He had to be hiding something, but he didn't give any clues as to what. Did he know who Rose was working with? Or was he involved with Brad's mom's mysterious fall outside her house?

Whatever it was, Brad was going to get to the bottom of it.

Chapter Twelve

BRAD YANKED the last weed out from under the rosebushes and stumbled back, nearly losing his footing.

He was paying more attention to his mom's conversation with Nancy Miller. His neighbor was older than his mom, but at the moment she seemed a lot stronger. She was talking about a new cat tree she'd gotten for her six pets. If she knew anything about Allison's murder, she wasn't saying anything.

The only reason Brad had insisted on going into the front yard with his mom, who wanted to work on the yard, was so he could get a feel for the neighbors.

So far, a half hour of weeding had only produced green under his fingernails.

Nancy stepped back and smiled at his mom. "It was delightful meeting you, Dianne. You're Brad's mom?"

Her tone made him tense. She was clearly saying it was surprising that someone so nice could be related to him.

"Yes," she said. "It was wonderful meeting you, too."

Nancy waved as she trotted off.

Mom turned to him. "Your neighbors are so great."

Brad turned and picked up a pile of weeds before she could see his expression and read his disagreement. One or more of them was a murderer. "Do you want me to get you another water bottle?"

"That would be fantastic. Thank you, sweetheart."

He dumped the debris into the yard waste container and headed inside, gulping down a water bottle before taking one out to his mom.

A moving van was backing into the driveway next door.

"Looks like you're getting new neighbors. Do you think they know about the poor boy next door?"

"I'm sure they do. Deaths are something realtors have to disclose."

She stepped closer. "I wonder if they know the details."

"Do you?" Brad scratched his head, trying to remember if he'd told her. He couldn't recall saying anything, but he had been under a lot of stress. Maybe he'd let something slip.

"Luna told me he was killed by a pretty woman. You really shouldn't let her in on such horrible details."

"It wasn't like that." He didn't feel like explaining that his coworker had kidnapped Luna.

After the moving truck parked, a white minivan pulled up to the curb and cut the gas.

"Looks like a family," she said. "We should introduce ourselves."

"I'm sure they don't want to be disturbed. Do you still want to attempt raking?"

"Yes. I only need one good arm for that." She marched over and grabbed the rake.

Brad looked around for more weeds, glad he'd distracted her from meeting the new neighbors. He wanted to scope them out first. Probably a family, given the minivan.

Children's laughter sounded from the other side of the moving truck, proving his point. At least it wasn't a young single guy. He wouldn't have to worry about his daughter's penchant for older men.

A thirty-something with an afro marched up the walkway followed by a woman who appeared slightly younger, wrangled three small kids, one who was strapped to her, flailing his arms and legs.

"You'll have to introduce yourself."

"Mom, you already said that."

She scratched her chin. "Did I? Well, you should. Those parents look downright exhausted."

He frowned. "You really don't remember saying anything?"

"Is it surprising, given the medications I'm on?"

She had a point. Her forgetfulness could just as easily be explained away by that.

Or it could be something else entirely.

Could the person framing him have gotten to her as a way to distract him? It wasn't out of the realm of possibility. He'd been jumped, framed twice, and his daughter had been kidnapped. Why not throw his elderly mother into the mix?

Anger churned, spreading throughout him. He turned before his mom could see his expression and yanked out weeds with renewed vigor. His mind raced as he tried to think of other things that could've been more than they seemed.

Hadley and Duke. The twenty-something had preyed on his oldest right under his nose. But why kill him? Wouldn't it serve their purpose to have him continue seeing Hadley? That would get under Brad's skin more than anything — he'd have killed the predator himself if Rose hadn't done it for him.

Although framing him for the murder had done a fantastic job of getting him off his game.

But what was the point in all of this? Whether it be someone from his neighborhood or someone from within BlueBlade? Who would hate him so much? Rose's excuse had been that she wanted to surpass him and make him pay for holding her back.

Seemed kind of weak. Or maybe she really was that shallow.

He didn't have any real enemies. Sure, certain people rubbed him the wrong way. People like Duke and his need to always be number one. But there wasn't anyone he had any real issues with.

However, if it was all tied together — the two people who jumped him, Duke and Allison's murders, Rose kidnapping Luna to lure him next door, and now his mom's unexplained injury — it had to be someone from BlueBlade. Nobody else would know he'd be after a target.

Brad leaned against a tree and wiped sweat from his brow. And now he was working from home. No way to look into the other assassins.

Unless he really did start working on the company website. There might be information stored about the employees. But that was probably a small chance. He didn't know much about websites, but that seemed an unlikely place to store highly sensitive information.

It would be on Kurt's computer. Or even his father's. Ralf didn't show up often, but in his seventies he still ran the operation. Kurt was not the top dog.

"Want to head inside?" His mom's voice pulled him from his thoughts.

"No. I'm just thinking."

"What about? You look like you're about to pop a blood vessel."

He studied her. "Tell me everything you remember about falling yesterday."

"This again?"

"Yes. What happened?"

"I really don't know. It's like I already told you and the doctors, I was walking out to the mailbox. Everything was normal until I found myself on the ground and my arm hurt horribly."

"Did you have Bingo with you?"

"No. I don't take him to get the mail. It's not long enough to be a walk."

"What about before?" Brad asked.

"Just a normal day."

"You didn't see anyone?"

"What do you mean?"

Brad frowned. He needed to tread carefully, or she could get really freaked out. "Nobody came to your door? Got a call from a wrong number?"

"What would that have to do with anything?"

"Did anything seem out of the ordinary before you left to get the mail?"

Her expression wrinkled. "What are you getting at?"

"People don't just fall and break their arm when the sidewalk is clear."

She rested her hand on her lower back. "This old body isn't what it used to be. You saw me stumble last night. I think this is my new normal."

"Did this new normal start yesterday? Or were there signs before?"

"Yesterday was the first time I've fallen, but we both know that when my lower back acts up it affects my knees. Something probably just went wrong with my back. I don't understand why you're making such a big deal about this."

"Have you been taking any new medication?"

"No. I don't want to talk about this anymore."

He drew a measured breath. "I'm trying to help."

"And I appreciate that, but there isn't some hidden mystery. I'm aging, and things aren't working like the once did. End of story." Her expression told him not to say another word.

He felt twelve years old.

"Brad," said a male voice from behind. "Is this your mother?"

His mom beamed, and they walked over to Lucas, who held his shaking little dog.

"I am." She held out her good arm. "I'm Dianne. And you are?"

"Lucas, and this is Mitzy. Pleasure to meet you, Mrs. Morris."

"Dianne, please." She patted the dog. "You're a little sweetheart. Too bad I don't have my Bingo out here. I bet they would make the best of friends."

"Oh, I'm sure you're right. As long as Bingo isn't a Great Dane."

They both laughed.

"No, he's a Lhasa Apso. Do you have a moment? I can go get him."

"I'd love that. Don't hurry on my account."

She headed for the house and Brad looped his arm through hers.

"I can do this on my own." She batted his arm away.

Lucas snickered. "You're a feisty one, aren't you?"

"Don't you forget it."

Brad made sure she got inside and then returned to Lucas.

"What has you so flustered?" Lucas set Mitzy down and adjusted her tiny, pink sweater.

"Too much going on." Brad raked his fingers through his hair.

"I see we have new neighbors. Have you met them yet?"

"No. They just pulled up."

Lucas stepped closer and leaned over the hedges separating them. "I don't know how they could live in a house where someone was killed."

Brad shrugged. "It's just a house."

"Where someone was brutally murdered."

"Murder isn't contagious."

Lucas shuddered. "But the energy left there would be like a black hole."

"There isn't anything magical about murder. What I'm concerned about is finding who killed Allison. Wes is hell-bent on it being me when I never left the party."

"Do you want to know what I heard?" Lucas glanced around and leaned closer.

"About Wes?"

Lucas hurried up the walkway and stood uncomfortably close to Brad. "You didn't hear this from me."

Brad nodded.

"There are whispers of him having a woman on the side."

"Really?"

"Yes. And I've seen him driving in and out of his house at odd hours, so I think it's a possibility."

"Have you told the police?"

"No."

"Why not?" Brad exclaimed.

"Because he drives around in the middle of the night and in the wee morning hours? That's not a crime."

"No, but if he was having an affair, he has motive."

"That's true."

"Was there ever anyone else in the car with him?"

Lucas shook his head. "Not that I saw."

"Who else thinks he was stepping out on Allison?"

"I can't tell you."

Brad threw his hands in the air. "That's not helpful! The detective keeps questioning *me*."

"I told you, you didn't hear it from me."

"So, now on top of everything else, I need to prove that jerk was cheating in his now-dead wife."

"I want to help you. I do. But Wes scares me. If he finds out I've been talking about him …"

Brad studied him. "Are you saying he threatened you?"

Lucas's eyes widened as he looked past Brad. "Is that Bingo? What a beauty!" He scooped up Mitzy and hurried over to the porch.

Brad wanted to pull his hair out. His neighbors were whispering about Wes's potential infidelity, but nobody would say anything even though it would help clear Brad's name?

The good news was, now he knew. He could still inform Detective Stewart. Then she could look into the other neighbors and find out who had seen what. But then again, she might not. She could easily say Brad was making it up to get the focus off himself — especially if he didn't give her any names.

Lucas left with Mitzy, waving to Brad.

He gave a half-hearted wave in return, barely able to pull himself from his thoughts.

His mom came over and nudged him. "Your new neighbors are out again. Let's go introduce ourselves."

"They don't want to be bothered while they're unloading boxes."

"It'll only take a minute, and they'll appreciate it. They'll also remember us — the first ones to say hi."

He sighed. Now that she had the idea in her mind, she wasn't going to let go. He may as well cave and meet his new neighbors. Then he could forget about them while he tried to figure out who was framing him for murder and possibly trying to kill him. Maybe he had two different people out to get him, people who were willing to hurt his family.

His mom tugged on his arm. He followed her to their driveway, his skin crawling. When he looked at the house, he flashed back to being helpless to get Luna from Rose. His mind also ran wild with images of what his older daughter had done in that house with Duke.

They reached the moving truck, just as the new guy was pulling out a plastic green box with a red lid.

He set it on a matching box and turned to Brad and his mom. "Hello."

"I'm Brad and this is my mom, Dianne. We're from next door." He nodded toward their house and extended his hand.

"Emerson." He shook their hands. "Pleasure to meet you both. My wife and kids are inside eating. I swear those kids are always hungry. I'll introduce you later."

"It's fine," Brad said. "We'll get out of your hair. I know you're busy."

"I'm glad you came over. Later, we can have a beer and get to know each other."

"Sounds great." Maybe this guy wouldn't be so bad after all. "I'll bring the drinks."

He hefted up the colorful boxes and nodded toward them. "Hope you guys like Christmas. Last year, my display was so massive it made one of the local news stations."

"Great." Brad forced a smile.

"Brad always decorates for the holidays." His mom smiled. "You two can share ideas."

"Or have a friendly competition." Emerson grinned.

"How about over dinner?" Brad's mom offered. "I'm sure you don't have the energy to make dinner. Come on over around six-thirty."

Brad turned to her. What was she doing?

Emerson glanced at Brad. "Are you sure?"

"I'll need to speak with my wife. Faye might—"

"Of course it's fine." His mom grinned. "Six-thirty."

"We'll see you then. Nice to meet you." Brad forced a smile and helped his mom down the driveway.

It was going to be a long night, and now he had to break the news to Faye that they were feeding an additional five people for dinner.

Chapter Thirteen

HADLEY STOOD FROZEN at her window, clinging to the curtains. Barely remembering to breathe every so often.

A new family was moving into Duke's house. It had been hard enough to watch his family show up and empty his house. She'd barely gotten past that.

Now he was being replaced. His memory covered by other people's things.

Did they know he'd been killed there? Or did they not care that the most amazing person ever to live had died within those walls?

She shook, and the growing lump in her throat made it even harder to take in air. Tears blurred her vision.

At least it was a family moving in. Maybe that would make it easier. If it was another single guy, it could be harder to deal with. But instead, there would be little kids growing up next door. That had to be good, right?

She'd spent most of her life here, and had primarily good memories. By the time they moved in, Dad was already working on his temper. Most of her bad memories were across town.

Until Duke's murder. Nothing beat that. That was, and always would be, the worst event of her life.

And now the world was moving on without Duke. It was like nobody cared. He couldn't experience anything anymore. Couldn't look outside and see the blossoms on the trees or the tulips poking out from the ground.

He would see nothing again. Touch nothing. Love nothing.

Gone.

And everything was moving on like he didn't matter. Even Hadley's life was pushing forward. But she would never forget him. That would never happen as long as she lived. Hopefully longer. She didn't want him ever removed from the collective consciousness.

She threw herself on her bed and let the tears flow freely. Wailed into the pillow. Screamed.

Not that it did any good.

It never did. Just relieved some of the pain for a little while, until it came back again. Some new memory, some jolting reminder.

Once she'd emptied her reserve of tears — again — she got up. Looked at her reflection.

Horrifying. She slunk into the chair and stared at the hot mess in front of her. Hair sticking out in every direction. Red, splotchy skin that matched her bloodshot eyes. Smeared makeup. Even dried snot.

It was a good thing nobody from school could see her. Though she didn't care much about her popularity status these days. And it showed, as the other girls were vying for her spot at the top.

She needed to pull herself together. But she needed to care first.

Maybe the new family moving in was a sign. Time to get back to life. Duke had wanted her to get the lead role for this new play, and she had. He was supposed to continue tutoring her singing.

Who was she kidding? He'd helped her advance to the point of not needing his help. It had gotten to the point where she practiced a few notes before their gazes locked and he pulled her close and they soon forgot all about the notes.

He would be so disappointed if she fell apart. There was no question he would've wanted her to go on and live her best life — and that was the exact opposite of the face staring at her from the mirror.

What she needed was another sign. Not just the family moving into Duke's space. If he really was trying to tell her to quit wallowing and feeling sorry for herself, she needed something else.

Hadley looked around her room. It was all normal. No signs from above.

Then an idea struck her. She pulled out her phone. If she opened her photos app and saw a happy picture of him, then that meant she was supposed to push forward. Give her all to the play, get her grades back up. She'd managed straight A's up to this point. Now several classes were in danger of breaking her streak.

Holding her breath, she unlocked her phone. She didn't even need to open the app. It was the last one she'd used. And the image on her screen was a selfie he'd taken while kissing her. He smiled at her with a devilish look in his eye while looking at her phone.

That was her sign.

It was officially time to pull herself together. Not that she couldn't mourn and miss him — that would never stop. Ever. Even if she did find another special someone one day, he would always be number one in her heart.

And besides, there was no way she could ever forget him. The world never would. She would make sure of that.

Hadley grabbed some fresh clothes and headed for the bathroom, keeping her head high and her back straight. If she acted happy and confident, she would soon feel that way.

As she got ready for a second time that day, she forced all of her heartache and worries to the side. Focused on things that needed to be done — studying for an upcoming quiz she was not prepared for, memorizing her lines, catching up on her other classes.

She almost felt normal when she stepped out of the bathroom.

Zeke stumbled up the stairs. "Did you see the new neighbors?"

"Go away." She reached for her doorknob.

"Grandma says they're coming over for dinner."

"Awesome."

"The dad is pretty young."

"Your point?"

He stepped closer, a smirk on his face. "Are you going to go after him, too?"

She stared unblinking. "How dare you."

"He's a good-looking guy. Probably not much older than Duke."

Hadley slapped him across his face.

His eyes widened, and he touched his reddening cheek. "You just hit me!"

"It was a slap! And you deserved it. Jerk."

Zeke's brows drew together. "Can't blame me for wondering."

"Can't blame me for slapping you." She balled her fists.

"You gonna punch me now?"

"Depends. Are you going to trash-talk me?"

"I was *asking* a question."

"You're being a jackass."

"Takes one to know one."

She flung open her door. "Leave me alone!"

He looked around and spoke loudly, a grin growing. "Are you afraid Mom and Dad are going to find out about Duke?"

"They already know." She stepped into her room and pushed the door.

Zeke blocked it, his mouth gaping. "They *know*?"

"Yes." She shoved the door. It didn't budge. The geek was stronger than he looked. "Go away."

"They seriously know?"

She glowered at him. "That's what I said, isn't it?"

"You didn't get grounded or anything?"

"What's the point? I'm already suffering enough. And he's dead, so it isn't like I can keep seeing him."

"Unbelievable."

"What are you talking about?" she demanded.

"You get away with *everything*."

"Excuse me?"

"You heard me!" Red colored his face as his brows furrowed. "I get busted for even thinking about doing something wrong, and you never get in trouble for anything. Even this!"

"Take it up with them." She shoved him, trying to get him out of the room.

"You'd better believe it. And be prepared. Once they see the error of their ways, you're going to get it."

She continued pushing against him, practically breaking into a sweat. "You have no clue what you're talking about."

Zeke stormed into the hall.

She fell against the wall and gave him an obscene gesture before slamming the door so hard it made her ears ring.

Hadley's heart pounded so hard, she was sure it would explode from her chest. Her stomach lurched. She was sure she'd puke, but deep breaths helped.

Through the door she could hear Zeke muttering. He kicked something, then stormed down the stairs.

She took unsteady steps to her bed.

Stared at it, breath hitched, before lifting the mattress.

Picked up the pregnancy test.

Still positive.

Chapter Fourteen

BRAD BREATHED a sigh of relief and placed the napkin on his plate. The dinner had gone off without a hitch. Faye hadn't even been upset about the added guests, and somehow his mom had been a huge help with the meal — despite only having one good arm.

Everyone fit at the now-extended dining room table that was only used for special occasions.

Faye stood and collected plates. "Who's ready for dessert?"

The younger kids all called out.

"You really didn't have to go to all this trouble," Cora said. "Dinner was more than enough."

Emerson put his arm around her. "I think what my wife is trying to say is thank you."

The adults laughed before taking the dinner dishes into the kitchen.

Faye pulled a cobbler from the oven.

Brad kissed her. "Thanks for being so gracious about my mom's invitation. I know we have so much going on already."

She checked the dessert's temperature. "It's a nice distraction, actually. I really like them, and Luna is thrilled to have younger neighbors so close. And I'm sure they're glad they don't have to cook after all that driving."

"Still, I appreciate it. Do you need me to do anything?"

"You can grab the dessert plates and some forks."

Less than five minutes later, everyone was digging in.

His mom set down her fork after just a bite. "My John was really into the Christmas displays, too."

"Really?" Emerson asked.

"Yes. Most of the time he decorated our house in the dark when it was late and often icy. He was a hard worker like my Brad. Two peas in a pod, those two."

Emerson smiled. "I look forward to working with Brad on a joint display this year."

"It'll be fun." Brad faked a smile. He was in way over his head if it was true about Emerson's display being on the news. His and Duke's decorations weren't anywhere near that good.

His mom leaned forward. "John used to work so hard. He would work fifty hours a week at his regular job, then spend an evening managing the car wash. It was a wonder we ever saw him."

Brad threw a worried look at Faye, but she was busy wiping some food from Luna's shirt. His dad hadn't worked a second job as a manager.

Maybe the ER doctor actually was onto something. He would have to keep a closer eye on things his mom said.

Cora smiled at her. "Your husband sounded like such a wonderful man. So much like Emerson. He would rather work overtime than let me do anything other than take care of the kids."

Emerson put his arm around his wife's shoulder. "Only

because she *wants* to focus on them. If she wanted to work, I wouldn't stop her."

Brad's mom beamed. "You're so much like John. I was always so proud of him and his drive to make sure we were taken care of. He'd never think of me working when providing for the family was his job."

Brad cleared his throat. "What do you do for a living, Emerson?"

"I'm an architect for a firm in California. When they gave us the opportunity to move here for the grand opening of our newest location, I jumped at the chance. Pine Harbor looks like a dream location."

Brad exchanged a knowing look with Faye before agreeing with Emerson. "It really is great. Not that you can ever *really* get away from some things."

Cora's smile faded. "You mean what happened in our house."

Hadley choked.

"Are you okay, dear?" Cora exclaimed.

Hadley nodded and drank some water. "Just went down the wrong way. You know about what happened?"

"Yes. They told us before we bought it."

"And you're okay with that?"

Emerson and Cora exchanged worried glances.

"Hadley." Faye glared at her.

"No, it's okay." Cora dabbed her mouth with a napkin. "We were a little surprised, but given the price, we couldn't turn it down. Our house in California was said to have been haunted, but we never experienced anything odd. This won't be any different."

"Did someone die there, too?"

"Hadley!" Faye turned to Cora and Emerson. "I'm so sorry."

"It's a normal question," Hadley said. "Pretty sure I'd

be concerned if that happened somewhere I was moving to, especially with kids."

Faye's nostrils flared.

"It's okay," Cora assured her and gave Hadley a half-hearted smile. "We see it as part of life — the most inevitable part."

"Being murdered in cold blood?"

"Hadley Marie!" Faye leaped up, pointing to the stairs. "Go to your room. Now!"

She stared at her mother.

"Was I not speaking English? To your room!"

"For asking questions?" Hadley's brows drew together.

"For being rude. Go."

"Fine." She marched to the stairs, leaving her plate on the table.

Faye drew in a deep breath. "I'm so sorry. Hadley's been going through a rough time lately. We try to be patient with her, but that was inexcusable."

"I don't mind. Really." Cora reached for another slice of cobbler.

"It's fine." Emerson gave her a reassuring smile.

"So, Brad tells me you like to decorate for the holidays?" Faye's voice was strained.

"Just Christmas." He grinned. "I've heard that airplane passengers can see my display when flying overhead."

"Daddy's lights were on the news." Liam beamed with pride.

Faye and Zeke both turned to Brad, obviously curious to see his reaction.

He smiled. "That's great. I can imagine you were quite proud that day."

"Oh, I was. I have the video and plenty of screenshots on social media."

Zeke grinned. "Duke used to get into the lights, too."

Emerson's grin faded. "The previous owner?"

"Yeah. He and Dad had this competition going. Everyone in the neighborhood knew about it."

"It was a *friendly* competition," Brad interjected. "And it wasn't a big deal."

Not like Emerson's display.

Emerson didn't seem to notice the shift in mood. "Fun. Maybe we can work together. You know, somehow connect the scenes. People would get a kick out of that."

"I'm sure they would." Brad forced a smile.

"Brad's father used to love Christmas lights," his mom said. "We would drive miles out of our way to see the neighborhoods with the best displays. That's how Brad got the bug to do it up once he got his own place."

Emerson shared some websites with Brad that had great deals on lights in the off-season, and before long, they were planning their united display that was eight months off. The road in front of their houses was sure to be as bright as a summer afternoon by the time they were done setting everything up.

The kids bounded to the playroom and the women made their way to the living room, laughing about something.

Before long, the new neighbors left for their own home, assuring Faye and Brad they would have their family over as soon as they were settled in.

After everything was put away, Faye handed Brad a glass of wine. "I'm worried about Hadley."

"More than before?"

"You saw the way she spoke to Emerson and Cora. It was embarrassing."

"Given everything she's been through, I think she's acting perfectly normal."

Faye gave him a double-take. "You're taking her side?"

"I'm not taking anyone's side, and I definitely don't like what she went through with Duke, but I can't blame her for being antsy about new people moving in. If something ever happened to you" — he shuddered — "I'd probably be irrational, too."

"So, you agree she was out of line."

"Of course, but I don't think it's anything to worry about. We can talk to her about being more thoughtful around the neighbors if it would make you feel better."

"She needs to know that's unacceptable."

"You already told her that much."

Faye took a long sip of her wine, and they settled into a silence.

Brad's mind wandered from Christmas lights to people who could want to frame him to the likelihood of his mom's broken arm not being an accident. He rinsed out his empty cup, kissed Faye, and headed to the backyard where his mom was watching Bingo smell everything in sight.

"Don't be too hard on Hadley. It's rough for kids at that age."

"I know, Mom." He considered his wording, how to breach the conversation about her medications. "How many pills are you taking?"

"Why?"

"I want to make sure you aren't overdoing it."

She frowned. "I'm not taking more than the doctors have prescribed."

"I know, but doctors don't always take potential inter-actions in mind. They should, but they don't. Remember when that one doctor gave Dad something for his back that gave him a seizure because it was taken with something else?"

"How could I forget?" She whistled. "Bingo, hurry up!"

"Are you sure nothing you're taking interacts badly with something else?"

"Dr. Kennedy checked my medications the last time I was in."

"But you haven't seen her since you've been to the hospital. When did she go over all of your medications?"

"I don't remember. Why are you making such a big deal about this?"

"I'm not. Did she go over them before you fell? Or have you added anything new to the mix?"

She called for the dog. "It's too much to think about. I'm going to bed."

"Have you started taking anything new recently? Before you broke your arm?"

"You're making too much of it. I appreciate your concern, but you need to back off. I can take care of myself. I've been doing that since you were sixteen."

"And look where that's gotten you." He gestured toward her cast.

"*One* accident." She let Bingo inside before marching after him.

He sighed and followed her. "You're sure nothing else got slipped in?"

She turned around and furrowed her brows. "How would that happen?"

"I'm just asking a question. Are you sure?"

"I trust my doctor. She isn't going to lead me wrong."

"Someone else could."

"How? She's the one who writes the prescription. Who else is going to get in there and mess with them? And more importantly, why?"

"There are any number of people with access to your medications between the doctor and the pharmacist."

"What would be the purpose in trying to hurt me? What have I done to any of them?"

He gritted his teeth. "This world doesn't run on what's fair or right. People have their own motives, and they don't care who they hurt to get what they want. I'm trying to make sure that hasn't happened to you."

She shook her head. "And you all think I'm the crazy one."

"We don't think you're crazy."

"You think I have dementia."

"I don't. That's what the doctor at the hospital said. We just want to take care of you."

"So, you aren't looking for symptoms of my memory failing?" She stared him down.

"More like, looking for proof that nothing's wrong."

"You didn't like what I was saying about your dad at dinner."

Brad hesitated.

"What?"

"I don't remember him working as a manager at nights."

"It was only one night every week or two for extra income," she said. "You were so busy with school and Faye, you probably didn't notice. And he didn't like to draw attention to himself. He did what needed to be done and didn't make a fuss."

"I didn't notice my father having a second job?"

"It was only one or two nights a month, and you were always out with Faye or your friends."

He thought back to his high school days before Dad passed away. He *had* been absorbed in his own life, but to miss something like that seemed odd. "Maybe."

Her expression softened. "Regardless, nobody has done anything with my prescriptions. I'd know."

"Will you humor me and let me have a look?"

"Nobody ever warned me of the day my son would treat me like a child." Her shoulders slumped.

"That isn't what I'm doing! I just want to look."

"Then you'll drop this nonsense and let me get back to healing and enjoying my grandchildren?"

"Yes."

"Have at it. I'm going to fix myself some tea. Would you like some?"

"No thanks."

She studied him a moment before heading toward the kitchen with Bingo trotting after her.

Brad leaned against the wall and muttered to himself, his muscles aching. Why did everything have to be so difficult these days? Hopefully, once he got to the bottom of it all he could rest easy. Take his family on that vacation the therapist recommended. That last session felt like eons ago. At this point, he wasn't even sure what day it was.

He marched upstairs, finding himself whistling along with the Aerosmith song coming from Zeke's room. At least he'd managed to pass on good taste in music to his son, if nothing else.

Once he got into the guest room, it didn't take long for him to find his mom's medications. Everything looked legit — not that he was an expert. He pulled out his phone and looked each one up. They were all for normal things like osteoporosis prevention, blood pressure, and that type of thing.

But did the pills match up? Had something been switched out? He opened one bottle and checked the color and shape of the pill to what he'd found online.

The door flung open.

"What are you doing?" Faye exclaimed.

"Checking my mother's medicines."

"That's what she told me, but I didn't believe her."

Brad closed the little bottle and opened the next. "Why not?"

"You're right. I should have. You've been acting a little crazy."

He shot her a glare while checking the tablets against what showed on his screen. "You really believe that?"

"Yes. It's no wonder Kurt gave you time off."

"I'm working from home."

"On what?"

"The company website."

She cocked a brow. "Really?"

"Yes. I've been a little busy with everything else going on, but that's what I'm doing."

"You? The same guy who needs his teenager to reboot his laptop?"

"Like you never ask Zeke for computer help." He narrowed his eyes at the little screen and held it up. "Would you say this is the same color as these pills?"

"You're impossible." She turned back for the door.

He set the bottle down. "I've never been saner. You know the type of people I deal with. What if the same person framing me has gone after my mother? It's hardly out of the realm of possibility. They've killed two of my neighbors and Luna ended up kidnapped. And now my mother tripped over *nothing* and broke an arm, only to be treated by a doctor who says she's showing signs of dementia when really she isn't. My whole life reeks of collusion! Someone is out to get me — and therefore everyone close to me — and that should scare you."

Faye sighed. "Luna went next door with someone she knew you worked with. It was a misunderstanding. And your mom is getting older. It's the cycle of life. Time for the younger generation to care for the older."

"That's really all you think is going on?"

She came over and rubbed his shoulders. "I think you're under a lot of stress and not thinking clearly. It could happen to anyone."

"That's where you're wrong."

And he would prove that to her and to everyone else. Hopefully, before anyone else got hurt.

Chapter Fifteen

FAYE STUCK the last breakfast dish into the washer and started it. She checked on Luna in the living room, who was watching a cartoon with Dianne and petting Bingo. Upstairs, music sounded from behind both teenagers' doors. Oingo Boingo for Zeke, and something she didn't recognize for Hadley.

She checked their room for Brad, but it was empty.

His office door was closed. No surprise there. Especially now that she knew the true nature of his job.

Faye shuddered at the thought. Could she ever get used to the fact her husband was a killer? Granted, as he always pointed out, he killed the bad guys. The people who escaped the justice of the law. But still, the same hands that caressed her also took men's last breaths. Women's too?

A cold chill ran down her spine. She always imagined disgusting old men. But women also committed murder. Had he killed one? Or multiple? How close did he have to get to do the deed? Did he press them close? Smell their perfume? Stare into their eyes?

She closed her eyes and shoved the thoughts from her mind.

They popped back up. This time, the women were younger, more attractive, less clothed.

Faye thought of kittens. Her children as babies. Puppies.

There was so little she knew about that side of her husband. She wasn't sure she wanted to know. But she also couldn't keep torturing herself with the wanderings of her imagination.

Brad's voice sounded from the other side of the door. Was he planning another killing? Or still searching for evidence that someone was plotting against his mother? Or was he really working on that website?

She inched closer. Cupped her ears. Heard him speaking, but couldn't make out any words. Pressed herself against the door, careful not to make a sound. The music from the kids' rooms was making it hard to hear anything.

Faye plugged her exposed ear and pressed her ear around, trying to hear anything. Given the natural pauses, he was having a conversation. Talking to Kurt? Another assassin? On a video call with a bunch of legal killers, discussing the newest tactics?

"… prescription drugs … pharmacy … watching the …"

She relaxed. He was only looking into Dianne's medicines. Now after letting her mind go crazy, that seemed so harmless. If he wanted to look into that, who was she to question him? Sure, it made no sense that someone would go to all the trouble of messing with a harmless old lady's prescriptions to get to Brad, but if it let him feel like he was doing something useful, why should she bother interfering?

Faye started to step away when she heard a word that made her stop cold.

"… Rose …"

Her heart skipped a beat. Maybe she'd misheard.

She had to have. Why would he be talking about — or worse, *to* — her?

No, now she was the one losing her marbles. Rose was in jail. She'd tried, and failed, to interfere with their marriage. Lured their young daughter away to try and kill Brad.

He wouldn't be talking to or about her. Not unless he was trying to figure out who was framing him. Then it would make sense to talk about her. She was in jail for just that.

Faye's pulse drummed in her ears with more vengeance than the AC/DC coming from Zeke's room, making it impossible to hear anything her husband said.

She pulled herself away from the door and wrung her hands together. She needed to get a grip. To trust her husband. There was nothing intimate going on between him and anyone he killed or had worked with — or anyone else, for that matter.

Her own nerves were on edge. That was it. Her friend had been killed not that long ago and now Allison's husband was blaming Brad. Their oldest daughter had been sleeping with the man next door. Now her mother-in-law was injured and living with them.

She was holding everything together quite phenomenally considering her life.

The doorknob jiggled.

Faye leaped away from the door and tried to look natural.

Brad stepped out and gave her a quizzical expression. "Everything all right?"

"No. Nothing is." She frowned. "Who were you on the phone with?"

"Were you listening in?"

"Stop being so paranoid. Besides, you think I could hear anything over this?" She waved toward Zeke's door muffling the blaring music. Hadley's was no longer playing.

"How'd you know I was on the phone?"

Busted.

"I heard you talking, that's all. I don't anymore." That much was true.

He turned his back to her, and she could hear him punching in his lock code. "I was talking to the detective."

"She's still on your back?"

"I called her." He turned around.

"Why?"

"Some things don't add up with Rose."

She'd been right. He had been talking about her. "Rose?"

"I'm obviously being framed, and that means it can't be her. She couldn't have killed Duke."

"You told Stewart you think you're being framed?" Faye exclaimed.

"Of course I did. I also told her the neighbors are all whispering about Wes cheating on Allison. That gives him motive. He had to have killed them both."

"What did he have against Duke?"

"I don't have proof of anything, but Rose has to be innocent."

"Or she wasn't working alone, and her partner killed Allison. You should be looking at people in your work."

"Believe me, I am. I'm looking at every possible angle."

"What if she was working with Wes?"

Brad lifted a brow. "Why would a trained assassin work with someone who can barely open a pocketknife?"

"Why would she be at the bar with him that night you showed up there?"

STACY CLAFLIN & NOLON KING

"She was trying to help me figure out who killed Duke." His eyes lit up. "See? Rose didn't kill him. She was trying to help me."

Faye tried to keep up with her racing thoughts. "The woman was framing you. Wes tried to make me think you were seeing her. It all fits together. She was working with him. That even fits with the fake pregnancy."

"How?"

"Think about it. If Allison knew about Wes's affair, she could've been pretending to be pregnant to keep him from leaving. He would think he'd have to pay child support for another kid, and for the next eighteen years."

Brad frowned. "But that's assuming he didn't know she was faking. How would that be possible? I mean seriously, they were married."

"But if he was cheating, they wouldn't have had much of an intimate life. She could've easily hidden it from him. It would've been even easier given that she would've been furious about the infidelity."

He looked up at the ceiling for a moment. "That does make sense. And if she was using the new baby as a way to keep him from leaving, it would give him all the more motive to kill her."

Faye's stomach lurched. "That's so messed up."

"The only thing I don't understand is him leaving the fake belly." Brad scratched his head. "Why leave proof of what she was using against him? That only makes him look all the more guilty."

"Except that everyone thought she was expecting. He could hardly get rid of it."

He snapped his fingers. "Actually, it *does* make sense. If he was so pissed about her holding the pregnancy over him, of course he would shred the fake stomach. Imagine the anger he would have toward it."

Faye took a deep breath and leaned against the wall, taking it all in. "That's what you should tell the detective."

"I'll let her figure it out. That's her job. I need to figure out whether Rose and Wes were working together. I need to know if the murders are linked. Was Allison's murder a rage killing, or did Wes have help from a trained killer?"

"It sounds like a coincidence to me." Faye raked her hands through her hair. Had her friend really been faking the pregnancy to keep her cheating husband from leaving?

"One thing I've learned is that there are no coincidences. But I'm glad we figured out this link. Thank you." He kissed her before returning to his office.

Faye stared in disbelief at the closed door.

If Wes did kill Allison, then it made all the more sense why he was trying to put the blame on Brad. He wasn't a husband looking for justice — he was a killer who needed someone to take the fall.

Brad really was being framed for a second murder, even if the two were unrelated.

Chapter Sixteen

HADLEY STEPPED BACK from her door, covering her mouth, hardly able to believe what she'd just overheard. Wes had been cheating on Allison and killed her because she'd faked her pregnancy to keep him from leaving?

That was crazier than the drama she was binge-watching when she couldn't sleep — which was pretty much every night.

She needed to tell Nate everything. They needed to get to the bottom of this.

They were his parents. He'd know if her parents' theory was possible. Or would he be in denial?

No. He'd want to get to the bottom of it. His mom's killer needed to be caught — even if it was his own dad. He would see that.

She grabbed her phone and texted Nate.

Hadley: Need to talk.

Nate: Now?

Hadley: Yes.

Nate: I'll call u.

Hadley: Not over phone.

Nate: Where?

Her mind raced. Where would be a good place to talk that nobody could overhear them?

Dots danced on the screen.

Nate: The park?

Hadley: Perfect. Be there in five.

Nate: OK.

Excitement ran through her. If they could figure out what really happened, then her dad would be off the hook. The detective could turn her attention to Wes and work toward actually solving the crime.

She checked her reflection and grabbed a few things before rushing out. Made it outside without running into anyone. Rain drizzled down, so she grabbed a coat and pulled the hood up and tightened it, then hurried the three blocks to the park.

There were a couple diehard joggers there, but nobody else. It was the perfect place to meet. No sign of Nate, though.

She leaned against a maple tree, protected from the incessant water drops. A few minutes passed before Nate appeared.

He wore black pants and a hoodie, kicking pebbles as he trudged along.

Hadley grew tired of waiting and jogged over.

"What's so important that it couldn't wait?" he asked.

"I've been thinking about your mom's killer."

"Do you think it's your dad?"

"What? No. Let's go sit at that covered bench. We're getting soaked."

Nate shoved his hands in his pockets and shrugged. "Sure."

She hurried over to the bench and waited for him to catch up. "Why'd you ask if it was my dad?"

"Seems to be what everyone's saying."

"It's not him. And once we prove that, we'll clear his name *and* get justice for your mom."

"What makes you so sure he didn't do it?"

"Are you kidding? I thought we were on the same page about this. You apologized for your dad showing up at my house, accusing my dad."

Nate stared into space. "Maybe he has a point. I mean, he didn't need to act like that, but your dad had motive for both Duke and my mom."

Hadley's mouth fell open. "Shut up."

"Think about it."

Her skin grew hot. "Your dad has more motive than mine!"

His nostrils flared. "My dad *loved* my mom. He's torn up over her death! Your dad couldn't stand her. It was obvious. He also didn't like Duke, because he was young and cool, and was always showing him up. Besides, if he knew you were doing the dirty with him, he would definitely want Duke dead."

It took all of her self-control not to punch him. "How dare you? What the hell has gotten into you? And for the record, *nobody* knew. They were all clueless."

"How dare me? You're accusing *my* dad."

She started to point out the obvious, but then closed her mouth. Of course he wouldn't want to hear her theory about his dad killing his mom. How could she have been so stupid to think he would be happy? With his mom dead, now his dad was all he had left — no matter what he'd done. Where would Nate and his siblings go if Wes went to prison?

"Well?" Nate's eyes narrowed.

Her mind raced for something to say that would calm

him down, or at least change the subject. "Do you know why your mom was faking her pregnancy?"

"I swear we already had this conversation." He rubbed his eyes. "Or maybe it was someone else. I can hardly keep up on who has been prying into my life lately." He looked at her. "They were trying to adopt and didn't want anyone to know they couldn't have kids."

"Couldn't have kids? But they have three."

"Put the pieces together, Hadley. We're all adopted."

She gave him a double-take. "You are?"

"Yes."

"You never told me that."

"That's because it's a taboo topic. We were each told the truth as little kids, then instructed never to breathe a word to anyone."

She let the reality soak in. If Wes did kill his wife, then their kids wouldn't be left as orphans. They would all have biological families they could return to.

It was perfect. She wouldn't ruin his life if they did prove Wes guilty.

They would all be fine, and a killer would be behind bars.

"Do you have anything else to say?" Nate asked. "Or can I go home now?"

She didn't want to drop the topic, but he was obviously in a bad mood. Plus, she needed to think about everything in this new light. "I'm not forcing you to stay."

Nate rose. "I gotta go. My dad's being pissy, and he's only going to get more furious if I don't clean the bathroom."

She stood, too. "Let's meet up later. When's good for you?"

"I don't know. Given the mood he's in, I might not be able to leave the house until school tomorrow morning."

"What a jerk."

"He's not a jerk!" Anger shone in his eyes.

Hadley jolted. "Okay."

Nate marched away.

"Text me!"

He didn't respond.

She watched him, trying to make sense of the conversation. He wasn't acting himself at all. Maybe he was just in a bad mood because his dad was being a jerk.

Once he disappeared from sight, she tightened her hood around her head and trudged back, ignoring the rain that was now soaking through her clothes.

She had to tell her parents that she'd overheard them and that she'd learned all of the Campbell kids were adopted. They sure acted like they were just a normal family. It was so weird that Allison would wear a fake pregnant stomach. Had she done that with all of her kids? Why not just embrace the beauty of adoption and tell everyone that was what they were doing? It wasn't like it was shameful. Hadley herself had often thought she'd like to adopt one day. Of course, she wanted to have her own kids — she'd never planned on it so young.

Now she was faced with her own decision. She was trying not to think about it, but it wasn't a problem that would go away by ignoring it. And it was Duke's baby, too. The one connection left to him. She couldn't get rid of it. That'd be like killing him all over again. That meant either keeping it or giving it up for adoption. Keeping it would mean no college.

What if it went to a family like Wes and Allison? She couldn't allow that.

There was no easy answer. But at least she had time to think about it. Nine months. She could even wait to hold it in her arms to decide. She wouldn't be one of those rude mothers who got some childless couple's hopes up about adoption just to change her mind and crush the couple after giving birth. She'd seen that happen, and it was lower than low. That wasn't her. She would never do that to anyone.

She wouldn't show for a long time, so she could focus on this whole Wes thing before worrying about this. As long as she forced herself to eat in front of her parents — sometimes the thought of food made her gag, but other times she couldn't get enough — then she could hide her problem and figure out what to do later. The summer was coming up before her stomach should start expanding. That'd be the perfect time to think things through.

Now there were more important matters, like helping to prove her dad's innocence.

Hadley turned down a street, trying to stay under as many trees as possible. The rain was really coming down and she was still more than a block away from home.

Wes stepped out in front of her from behind a bush, his face contorted in anger.

A scream caught in her throat.

He said nothing, just stared at her, blocking her way.

"E-excuse me." She stood taller, pretending not to be as intimidated as she was.

"What do you think you're doing?"

"Walking. Not that it's any of your concern."

His eyebrows furrowed. "Were you talking to my son?"

She wanted to say something about Nate being adopted, but she restrained herself. "Does it matter?"

Wes leaned forward, his face so close she could smell beef on his breath. "You need to stay away from my family. Do you hear me?"

Her heart pounded and tears threatened, but she stood

unblinking. "I can be friends with anyone I want to be. And Nate is old enough to make his own decisions, too."

Wes poked her shoulder. "You stay away from us, or you'll be sorry."

"Don't touch me!" She looked around to see if anyone heard her.

Nobody was in sight.

He took a step back. "I'm serious. I don't want my kids anywhere near Brad's spawn."

Hadley's mouth fell open. "You didn't just say that."

Wes got in her face again. "I did, and you'd better take heed."

"And you'd better not touch me again." She stared him down.

He stormed away.

She shook, trying to catch her breath.

Take heed? Who talked like that?

He *had* to be guilty of Allison's murder.

Once she was sure she wouldn't burst into tears — her emotions were all over the place lately — she hurried home. In her room, she dug through a box of knives Dad had given her through the years. All BlueBlade, of course.

Hadley found the largest pocketknife and shoved it in her pants pocket. The next time Wes blew his beefy breath on her, she would pull it out and show him she was not someone to mess with.

Chapter Seventeen

"You sure you got everything?" Faye glanced at her mother-in-law's house.

Dianne had wanted a few more comforts from home and ended up filling two boxes.

Faye's stomach knotted as she wondered how long Dianne planned on staying with them. At the hospital, they'd planned on something long-term, but she hadn't shown signs of dementia like Faye had expected. Dianne knew who they all were and was able to take care of herself quite well considering she had a broken arm. All of that gave *some* credence to Brad's suspicions about it not being an accident, so Faye had started to think the stay wouldn't last very long.

Dianne rifled through the boxes. "That should do. But we can always come back to get more later."

Faye smiled and helped her mother-in-law into the car. "Let me check your mail, since we're here."

On the way to the box, she glanced around for anything that might've tripped her up, causing her to break her arm.

It was like Brad mentioned. There was nothing. The sidewalk was clear.

She gathered the envelopes, handed them to Dianne, and started the car. The ride home was in relative silence as Dianne went through her bills and magazines.

As she turned down their street, Brad's car was pulling out of the driveway. She held her hand up to wave as he passed, but he went the opposite direction than usual.

"Where's he going?" Dianne asked.

"I'm not sure." Faye whipped out her phone and voice commanded a text.

After a few seconds, it still hadn't been read, so she pressed the gas.

"Where are *we* going?"

Faye clutched the wheel, hoping she could catch up to him. He had already turned and was out of her line of sight. "I want to find out where Brad's headed. He told me he was going to be in his office all afternoon."

"He probably has to work. John was the same way — running to the office every moment they needed him. He was such a good provider. He even had provisions set up. Even though he died so long ago, I've never been without. I don't know how he did it, but our Morris men are good men."

"They sure are." Faye craned her neck, trying to catch a glimpse of Brad.

His black Mercedes was just around the corner.

Her breath hitched, and the tires squealed a little as she made the turn.

"What's the rush?" Dianne made a show of clutching her purse with her good arm.

"He isn't answering his texts."

"My boy knows better than to text and drive."

Faye held back a snort. That was one thing her

mother-in-law was wrong about Brad. Texting and driving had been a point of contention between the two of them. Though it had gotten better, he still did it. But now it made sense — he thought he was above the law because his position at work actually *was* above the law.

She was closing the distance between the two cars, so she let off the gas, focusing on the black sedan up ahead.

Brad not only left the neighborhood the back way, he turned toward the freeway.

He was heading out of town, and not even letting her know where he was going.

Something was definitely up. It was a good thing she followed him.

A few minutes later, Brad got on the on-ramp.

She'd been right.

Where was he going?

Dianne changed the station and turned up the music when she got to a 60s song.

Faye resisted the urge to lower the volume. Though she wanted silence to follow Brad, it was unreasonable to ask Dianne to sit in quiet on a road trip she didn't ask to go on. And at least it kept her from talking. That would be too much of a distraction.

She checked her phone repeatedly, seeing if Brad read or responded to the text.

He hadn't.

They stayed on the freeway for five miles, ten miles, fifteen.

Where on earth were they going?

If they didn't stop soon, Faye would have to call home and let Hadley and Zeke know to fix Luna something to eat.

Just as she was about to send Brad another text, he

turned on his blinker. He was finally getting off the freeway.

She didn't recognize the exit, so the destination was a mystery.

"Are we going to stop for some food?" Dianne asked.

"We might have to." Faye followed Brad on the off-ramp, staying back as far as she dared.

They traveled down a few main roads of what appeared to be a small rural town. If there was a sign with the name, she'd missed it. Then Brad turned down a winding, narrow road with nothing other than farm animals and fields of grass.

Then after what felt like a dozen more turns, a large cement structure loomed ahead. It sprawled for acres and had a tall fence surrounding it with towers on each corner.

A prison.

Brad turned and stopped at the gate. Was let in immediately.

Honk!

She waved an apology to the driver behind her and pulled over, watching as her husband's car made its way to the parking lot. Then he marched toward the building.

He still hadn't read her text.

There was only one person he could be going to visit.

Rose.

Her stomach knotted.

"What's Brad doing there?" Dianne asked.

"Visiting someone from work." She didn't pull her gaze from Brad.

"Do they sell knives to the prison guards?"

"Yeah."

"I wouldn't have thought that, but it makes sense."

Knock, knock!

Faye startled and looked over to see a uniformed officer

knocking on the passenger window. She rolled down the window. "Can I help you, officer?"

"You need to leave, ma'am. Either drive on, or come in if you have business, but you can't idle outside the property."

She glanced behind him. Brad wasn't in the parking lot. He must've already gone inside. "I understand. Thank you."

"What are you doing out here?" He stepped closer to the vehicle.

Faye cleared her throat. "Just looking. I'll be on my way. Didn't mean to cause any problems."

He started to say something, but she rolled up the window and pulled away, scanning the building as she drove. Tried to ignore the pangs of jealousy. They were ridiculous. Brad had no interest in Rose. He was a dedicated family man. He loved Faye. Only Faye.

Images of him eating at the bar with Rose pushed their way to the front of her mind.

Why would he go and visit her while ignoring her texts?

She would have to find out later since she wasn't allowed to watch the building. Besides, she needed to take Dianne home and start making dinner. The kids would be famished before long.

Faye drove a little farther before turning around. Then she kept her speed low, keeping her focus on the prison. Not that she expected Brad to step out so soon. He probably hadn't even made it to see Rose yet.

Rose.

Her blood boiled, pulse pounded.

She squeezed the steering wheel so tightly her knuckles turned white. Took deep breaths.

Brad was only visiting her to find a killer. Nothing more

— even if it felt like so much more. And it did. She wanted to punch something.

"Faye?"

She jumped, having momentarily forgotten she wasn't alone. "I'm fine."

Once she made the first turnoff from the road leading to the prison, she pulled over.

"What are we doing now?" Dianne asked.

"I need to make a phone call." And also to wait and see how long it took for Brad to return, assuming there wasn't an emergency at home.

Dianne sighed and opened one of her magazines. "I'm going to have to eat soon. Do you have anything in the car?"

"Check the glove compartment. I usually keep snack bars for the kids."

Dianne pulled one out.

Good. That should keep her content for a while. Hopefully long enough.

Faye called Brad. Straight to voicemail.

Called Hadley. Also voicemail. But she sent a text afterward.

Hadley: Cant u text like a normal person?

Faye: I want to talk. Call me.

Hadley: U can text it just as easy.

Faye gritted her teeth.

Faye: I'm going to be a while. Is Luna OK?

Hadley: We're all fine. See how easy that was?

Faye: Thinking of picking up pizza. Sound good?

Hadley: Perfect! C u soon.

Faye: Bye.

She tried Brad again, getting the same response.

Waited a while.

A police cruiser approached.

Why couldn't they leave her alone? She wasn't doing anything wrong.

Reluctantly, she pulled into traffic and headed for the freeway. She would have to wait to speak with Brad until whenever he finally showed up at home.

Chapter Eighteen

BRAD TAPPED the table and looked around the tiny room with multiple windows for officers to look in. There was probably even a listening device somewhere, not that he could see one. He'd been checking.

If only he could discuss his high level in the government — higher than any of the guards telling him what he can and can't do while inside the prison. But that was the way it went. Law enforcement couldn't know about what they did.

After what felt like days, the door finally opened. Two large guards shoved a handcuffed Rose inside. It was strange seeing her like that after having spent so much time training her and seeing her in action. Without the cuffs, she could take down both the officers, armed or not.

So could Brad, for that matter. But he had to restrain himself. The most important rule of BlueBlade was not discussing the real purpose of the business.

One guard cuffed Rose to the table while the other forced her to sit in the chair.

"We'll be outside if you need us."

They left, slamming the door.

Rose sat up straight and glared at him. "What do you want?"

He studied her, finding her far less intimidating than last time, now in a jumpsuit and with no makeup and messy hair.

"Well?" Her expression hardened.

Brad looked around. "I don't buy your story."

"Meaning?"

"You said you wanted my position in the company."

"So?" She picked at a nail.

"I don't buy it. Why take such a big risk?"

She looked at him like he was an idiot. "Because you were supposed to go down. Obviously."

He shook his head.

"What?" Her eyebrows narrowed.

Brad held her gaze a moment. "You wouldn't risk your entire career."

"Shows how little you know me. I thought you knew I was a loose cannon. That's what everyone says."

"But you're also smart. You're not going to risk this" — he panned his palm around the room — "to take me down. You'd wait it out."

Rose shrugged. "I didn't give you enough credit. I got caught. That's the way it went down."

He squared his shoulders. "I don't think you did it."

"No?"

"No. I believe this outcome surprised you as much as it did me."

"That's where you're wrong. It's all like I said back in Duke's kitchen." She rested her chin on her hand. "I underestimated you, and here I am."

"The story is, you were seeing Duke. We both know that's a lie."

"Do we?" She yawned.

Anger burned in his chest. "Why are you doing this? I'm trying to help you!"

"Nobody can help me. Even if I were to get out, there's no going back to BlueBlade. *This* is my lot now."

"You can't mean that!"

"Again, why do you care? I tried to ruin your marriage, and here you are convinced of my innocence. Newsflash — all of my flirting was fake. I'm totally not into old guys."

The words were like a slap. "I'm not old."

She rolled her eyes and turned her attention back to her nail.

"I know you weren't seeing Duke, because I know who he was really hooking up with."

Rose glanced up, both brows raised. "He was seeing someone? Who?"

"Not important."

"You're such a tease." She smirked.

"Look." He pressed his palms on the table. "Someone killed Allison Campbell after you were arrested."

"Probably Wes. It's always the husband."

"My point is, somebody is framing me."

"You think?" She yawned again.

Brad balled his fists under the table but managed to keep his frustration off his expression. "And if that's the case, it's not you."

"*Do* you know that?"

"What?"

She sat up straight, her glare icy. "How do you know the person I was working with isn't continuing on with our plan to take you down?"

"After you're in here?"

Her nostrils flared. "Being arrested doesn't change how I feel about you. In fact, I'd love to see you in here with me."

Brad stared at her in disbelief. "Who are you working with?"

"You think I'd give him up?"

"Him. That narrows down half the options."

"Shut up."

It was his turn to smirk.

"It's only a matter of time until you're in here. Once that happens, I can prove my innocence."

"You're guilty as sin — you tried to kill me and you kidnapped my daughter. That alone will keep you in here, regardless of your involvement in Duke or Allison's deaths."

"You already said I can't be involved with hers."

"I'm sure you already had that plan concocted far in advance."

"Still eager to prove I couldn't be involved with your framing?"

He drew a deep breath. "You're making it easier to walk away. But I don't understand why you don't want my help. I'd think you'd jump at the chance to get out of here."

Rose turned her attention back to her nails. "I'm in for the long game."

Brad hesitated. "Meaning?"

She glanced at him through her lashes. "None-ya."

"Not my business? Are you serious?"

Her only response was to purse her lips.

"Don't want to tell me? Even though I could help you?"

"You have enough to worry about. Forget about me and focus on your family. M'kay?" She leaned back and crossed her arms.

He resisted the urge to rub his temples. "What does that mean?"

"Look, Brad. I didn't always despise you. There was a time I had stars in my eyes, thinking you were untouchable. But I've since wised up. You don't care about anyone else, and trust me when I say this, that's going to be your undoing."

"I care about plenty of people — but not you anymore. What's your point?"

Her expression softened. "I'm saying this to the guy who was once the father figure I needed at the time, not to the current you. Got it?"

Father figure? Ouch. He nodded, not showing any emotion.

She licked her lips and glanced to the side before turning her attention back to him. "You've burned a lot of bridges. If you think you don't need to watch your back, you're more arrogant than I ever thought possible. And that's saying something."

He clenched his jaw. "You're saying there are people within BlueBlade who want me dead?"

"I didn't say anything."

"Other than I should be looking within the company."

"Not what I said."

Brad leaned back and let the news settle. It wasn't like he had never suspected it could be an inside job — especially not with him being jumped during a hit — but now he had proof. If he could trust a word coming out of that woman's mouth.

"Are we done here?"

"So, I should get my focus off Wes."

"I said nothing of the sort."

His mind raced, trying to figure out who he had pissed off that bad. Enough to want him dead. "Is it someone higher up, or one of those young guys you hang out with?"

She picked at lint on her jumpsuit and whistled.

"Not going to say any more?"

Rose shook her head.

"Even though I could actually help you?"

She looked back at him. "I already told you I'm not the innocent dove you thought. Forget about me. Actually, drop this whole thing. You'd be a lot better off getting a hobby. Your obsessive nature is a big reason you're in this mess to begin with."

"I'm not obsessive."

"Whatever you have to tell yourself." She looked at the clock. "Are we done here?"

"Am I keeping you from something important?"

"Yeah, actually."

He pinched the bridge of his nose. Tried to remember if there was anything else he needed to ask her. If there was, it was pointless. She was either guilty or covering for someone in the company. Or she wanted him to *think* her co-conspirator was part of BlueBlade.

"I'm waiting." She tapped the table.

"Tell me one thing."

"What?"

"Is the person you're working with high in the company, or low?"

She snorted. "I'm not giving him up."

"I didn't ask for his name, but I do appreciate you reiterating that it's a him."

Rose leaned over the table, her nose inches from his. "If you think BlueBlade is the only game in town, you're thinking too small."

He jolted. "Wait, what?"

She sat up straight. "Guards, we're done!"

Brad grabbed her wrist.

"Don't touch me. I'll scream."

He pulled away. "Are you saying there's another front? Another company?"

Rose turned toward the door. "Guards!"

"Is there another company other than BlueBlade?"

The door opened, and the same two guards returned.

"Is there?" Brad demanded.

She met his gaze before giving a slight nod.

Confirmation.

The guards led her toward the door.

"Really?" he called.

Another nod.

Then they were gone, the door slamming between him and them.

Silence echoed.

Brad slumped in the chair and rubbed his temples.

There was another company like BlueBlade working as a cover for the assassination ring.

And Rose, new to the business, had knowledge of it. Was potentially working with someone from the other company against him.

Who else knew about it?

He needed to find out what it was and who worked there.

All without letting Kurt know.

Why had Rose told him? Did she actually want his help?

That had to have been her way of communicating it to him.

Now he couldn't trust anyone at BlueBlade. At least not

until he could prove whether another front actually did exist.

Either Rose or Kurt was playing him.

Maybe both.

He was going to find out.

Chapter Nineteen

BRAD PULLED into his driveway and leaned his head against the steering wheel, pressure building behind his eyes. He'd gotten no closer to answers by talking with Rose.

He had *more* questions now.

On the way home, he'd looked at what had to be half the businesses in Pine Harbor. Any one of them could be a cover for the assassination ring. A laundromat? Dry cleaner? Those seemed too obvious. But maybe that was the point.

The trick would be figuring out which one it actually was. What other business was Kurt actually running?

That certainly explained his boss being away from the office so much, beyond the obvious reason of keeping track of so many hits — both the perpetrators and the assassins.

Was the other business new? Or had it been in operation the entire time Brad had been with BlueBlade?

He needed to get into Kurt's office. That was easier said than done. A better first step might be to talk with the other assassins to see what they knew. Poke around and try to get someone to let something slip. Then if that didn't pan out, he would try breaking into his boss's office.

Brad popped a few ibuprofen before gathering his things and going inside.

Faye stood in the entry, her arms crossed.

"Did I do something wrong?" He hung his jacket on the coat rack and kicked off his shoes.

"I've been calling and texting you."

"It was on silent. I forgot to turn it back on." He pulled it out of his pocket and showed her, seeing over forty total notifications. His heart sank. "Was there an emergency?"

"No. Luckily." Her eyes narrowed.

"It was an honest mistake."

"Why did you visit Rose?"

He gave her a double-take.

"Yes, I know about that."

"How?"

"I followed you. I'm surprised you didn't notice, given your *training*."

"Not so loud!"

"What were you doing?"

He stepped toward her to give her a kiss.

She backed away, her mouth forming a straight line.

"I wanted to hear her side of the story."

"You didn't get enough when she was threatening to kill you?"

"No. I thought she might be innocent since she obviously couldn't have murdered Allison."

"And do you still think that?" Faye glowered at him.

Brad shook his head. "She admitted to working with someone, and that person is obviously running free."

"Are they trying to frame you?"

"It would appear so."

"Appear? You don't know?"

He took another step toward her.

She didn't back away.

"I didn't get as much information as I'd have liked. But at least I can stop worrying that an innocent person is behind bars."

"Why would you be concerned about her at all? She tried to kill you."

"Because I need to get to the bottom of this. The quicker the better. Can we talk upstairs?"

She backed away a few steps. "Are you hungry? We already had pizza. There's some left. We would've waited, but I couldn't get ahold of you, so I didn't know when you'd be home."

He ignored the jab and shook his head. "I don't want to eat. We need to talk in private."

"Fine."

They went up to their room. Brad locked the door and sat next to her on the bed. "She says there's another cover company."

"What does that mean?"

"BlueBlade isn't the only business in town covering for the assassinations."

She lifted a brow.

"The person framing me could be working at the other location."

"You believe her?"

"I have no reason not to, at least until I can prove she was lying."

Faye sighed.

"What's the matter?"

"I thought we moved past the Rose issue, but now we're right back here again."

"No, we aren't."

"You snuck off to see her."

Brad put his hand on her thigh. "I forgot my ringer was off. That's all."

"You didn't tell me where you were going."

"Because you weren't home when I left. Zeke was supposed to tell you I was leaving for work business when you got home."

"It wasn't his responsibility. You should've let me know yourself. It would've taken five seconds to send me a text."

He closed his eyes a moment to collect himself. "You're right. I wasn't thinking."

She scooted away. "We need to discuss this with Dr. Trellis."

"Why? It'll be impossible to discuss when we can't talk about the true nature of my job."

"You should've thought of that before sneaking off."

"I wasn't sneaking!" He took a few deep breaths to calm himself. "If I was trying to hide anything, do you think I'd have gone in broad daylight?"

"It was raining, but that's beside the point. I couldn't reach you, and you were spending time with Rose — who was already an issue."

"I never had any feelings for her. Ever."

"Doesn't change the fact of her flirting with you or you two being together at a bar."

"To discuss Duke's murder!"

"You know how it looked when Wes sent that photo to Allison. I can't forget that."

He got up and paced. "You said you understood. We moved past that!"

"I can forgive, but forgetting is another matter altogether."

"While I can appreciate that, I need you to trust me. I was serious when I told you that you're the only person for me. Always have been, always will be. You're my anchor, and I need you."

Faye's expression softened.

"Please remember that. No matter how things look — and given my business, some things could look really bad."

"They already have."

"Exactly. That's why I need your trust. Now more than ever. Someone is definitely trying to take me down, and chances are good it's not even anyone I know. My thoughts were on BlueBlade assassins. Now it could literally be anybody. I *have* to find out what the other storefront is."

She put her arm around him. "How are you going to figure that out?"

"I'm not sure — and that's a big problem. I don't know where to begin. Pine Harbor isn't a huge town, but there are a lot of businesses. Any one of them could belong to Kurt and Ralf."

"You never see Ralf anymore, right?"

"Correct."

"What if he runs the other store, and Kurt runs BlueBlade?"

"It's a possibility, but you have to remember Ralf is in his seventies. He isn't going to be very active."

Faye lifted a brow. "Don't be so sure. Remember my grandpa who played tennis in the Arizona heat every day until he was nearly eighty?"

"True. So, Ralf could be my ticket to finding out what's going on."

"Does he—"

Knock, knock!

Brad turned to the door. "Not now!"

"It's important," Hadley called from the other side.

He threw Faye a pleading glance.

"She did tell me she needed to discuss something with us when you got home."

Brad unlocked the door and cracked it open. "Can this wait? Mom and I are having an important discussion."

"No! This is life or death — literally."

He exchanged a glance with Faye.

She nodded.

Brad held back a groan and let their daughter in. "What's the emergency?"

Hadley stepped in and closed the door. "*All* of Wes and Allison's kids are adopted!"

"How is that urgent?"

She scrunched her face and looked back and forth between her parents. "I was eavesdropping when you guys were talking about Wes and Allison earlier. Then later, when I was talking with Nate he told me it was a huge secret. None of them are allowed to tell anyone."

Faye lifted a brow. "Yet he told you?"

"He knows things about me."

Brad's stomach dropped. "Duke?"

"Yeah."

Brad tugged on his hair. "You told him?"

"He's trustworthy."

"No! He's a Campbell."

Hadley glared at him. "He's not going to tell anyone."

"If he tells his dad, it's going to look like I had motive to kill Duke!"

"But Rose was arrested for that."

"Doesn't mean he can't point fingers. I'm sure there are people like him who think she couldn't have pulled it off alone. The next logical step is that people will think I could be guilty of killing Allison, who I didn't obviously hide my disdain for."

Hadley's eyes widened. "Oh."

"Yes. Oh." He paced again, his heart racing.

Things were spiraling.

Hadley said something, but Brad couldn't focus. Faye responded. Good. He needed to do something about this, and fast. Maybe she was onto something about the adoption thing. Why would Wes and Allison be so adamant about hiding that? It wasn't like fertility problems were rare. But to go so far as not letting the kids talk about it and faking a pregnancy? There had to be something there.

Although if Wes wanted to hide the whole adoption thing, leaving her shredded fake belly made no sense. It told the world what was going on, at least this time around.

Unless it was Allison who was adamant about keeping it all a secret. Maybe she thought it marred their image of the perfect family. And Wes, the cheating husband, could have disagreed with her. Been eager to come clean or to let the world know the burden she was placing on everyone in the family.

It did kind of make sense. But to go as far as murder? There had to be other issues at play. The quickest way to find out would be for Hadley to ask Nate.

Brad stopped pacing and turned to his daughter. "If you ask Nate more questions about his parents, do you think he'd answer?"

She shrugged. "He wasn't too eager to talk to me today. Plus, Wes made it clear he doesn't want me near his kids."

"What do you mean?" Brad exchanged a worried glance with Faye.

Hadley sighed. "On my way home after talking to Nate, Wes told me I better stay away from his kids or else."

"Or else?" Brad exclaimed. "Is that what he said? He threatened you?"

"Yes. No, he didn't say that exactly." She looked deep in thought. "He said I'd be sorry. That's what he told me."

"You'll be sorry? How?"

"He didn't say. But he did poke my shoulder, and I told him not to touch me. Then he called me your spawn."

Brad's blood boiled. "*He's* going to be the one who's sorry after I rearrange his face." He marched toward the door.

"What are you doing?" Faye demanded.

"I'm going to have a discussion with that lowlife."

She stood between him and the door. "Don't act rashly."

"Did you hear what he said to our daughter?"

"Yes. We need to think about how to handle this."

"My fist can think just fine — and get the message across quite clearly to leave my family alone."

Faye pleaded with her eyes. "People already suspect you, and if you beat up Wes, that's only going to convince everyone of your guilt. Besides, that's probably what he wants."

Brad hesitated. She did have a point.

"You'll wait?"

He turned to Hadley. "You'll stay away from Wes?"

"Of course. He's a creep."

Brad turned back to Faye. "I'll wait, but it's only a matter of time before I do confront him."

Chapter Twenty

HADLEY READ over the next line, but the words seemed to dance around. She took a deep breath and focused. The words were too blurry.

"Hadley?" said Mrs. Cowell.

She turned to her, but must have moved her head too fast because white dots danced around. "What?"

Several of the kids giggled.

"Your line."

"Right." Hadley turned back to the paper, her head feeling like it could float away. She managed to read the words. Held them in her mind as she turned to Emily. "My, how bright the sun shines this afternoon. It's like the—"

The white dots flooded her vision, blocking her view of Emily and the rest of the stage.

Laughter.

Then gasps.

Everything seemed to be moving.

Arms wrapped around her.

Something crashed. Her elbow hurt. It was hard to breathe.

"Hadley?"

She didn't recognize the voice. Couldn't see past the dots.

"Get her to the nurse's office!"

Hadley shook her head, managed to take in a deep breath. Some of the dots disappeared. Enough that she could see some of the other kids and the teacher.

Why was she sitting on the floor?

She focused on Mrs. Cowell. "I'm okay. Just got a little dizzy. I think I'm dehydrated. That's all."

"Emily's going to help you to the nurse's office."

"I'm fine." Hadley pulled away from Emily's grasp and tried to stand. Her knee gave out.

Tyler leaped over and caught her. "We'd better get you to the nurse. You're pale as a ghost."

Hadley scowled. "I'm fine. Give me some water, and I'll show you."

Mrs. Cowell shook her head. "If the nurse gives you the clear, you can come back and finish. Otherwise, go home and rest, sweetie."

Hadley tried to pull away from Tyler, but he was too strong.

Or she was too weak. Maybe this was more than being dehydrated.

Not that she would admit it.

Tyler kept his arm around her and guided her to the hallway.

"I'm fine, you know."

"Mrs. Cowell's right. You should at least get checked out. You were really pale back there."

"But I'm not now?"

He glanced at her. "Not as much."

She frowned.

"I don't know if you're doing that pineapple diet Lizzy

155

and her friends were talking about, but it doesn't sound good."

"I'm not on any diet. What is it with everyone lately? Do I look like I need to be on one?"

Tyler snorted. "Of course not. I'm just saying some of those weird diets sound dangerous to me."

Someone rounded the corner and nearly crashed into them.

Nate. His eyes widened, then his mouth curved into a sour frown. He hightailed it the other way.

"Did you steal his puppy or something?" Tyler asked.

Hadley almost smiled. "No. There's some stuff between our two families. Basically, his dad's being a jerk."

"Nothing new there."

"Really?"

"Yeah." Tyler stopped in front of the nurse's office. "Nate and I were best friends in the fifth grade, and his parents were cray-cray. They seem normal until you get to know them. It got to the point that my parents wouldn't let me go to his house anymore."

"Why not?"

He glanced at the time. "I'll tell you later. Mrs. Cowell is going to be mad if I'm not back to practice my lines."

Tyler helped her inside and told the receptionist what happened before waving to Hadley and leaving.

The receptionist asked her a few questions, to which Hadley responded that everyone was overreacting because she was just dehydrated.

Before she knew it, the nurse was taking her temperature and checking her vitals.

"This is all overkill. I just need water."

"Do you have any underlying health conditions that I should be aware of?"

"No."

"Are you sure?"

Hadley's heart hammered. No way she could know about the baby. She glared at the nurse. "You can look at my records. Nothing's wrong with me."

After a few more minutes of back and forth, and checking her over, the nurse wrote some stuff on a pad of paper. "Do you have a ride home?"

"I have a *car*."

"You shouldn't drive right now."

"Then give me some water, and I'll be fine."

She shook her head. "You passed out."

"I never lost consciousness. I was just lightheaded. Huge difference."

"You're still ashen."

Hadley made a mental note to pack snacks and make sure she always had enough to eat. Although at this rate, she wouldn't be able to hide her condition much longer.

But she would keep it secret as long as possible.

The nurse flipped through her file and made a phone call.

Hadley's breath caught. What was she doing?

"Is this Faye Morris?"

Hadley buried her face in her palms. Now her mom would know what was going on. She'd definitely freak out.

After getting off the phone, the nurse finally gave Hadley a bottle of water. "You can stay here until your parents arrive."

"What about my car?"

"They're both coming, so I'm sure one of them can drive it for you."

"I'm perfectly capable."

"Better safe than sorry. Stay here until they arrive." She hurried out, leaving the door cracked. The receptionist could look in and see her if she turned around.

No sneaking out.

Hadley grumbled and took a few sips of the water. It tasted horrible. Nothing tasted the same anymore. Chicken was the worst. She had to pretend to eat it when her mom made it. Luckily, Mom preferred other meats, and they didn't have it often.

She glanced at the receptionist, who was busy talking with some goth kid with a bloody piercing. Hadley tiptoed to the sink and emptied the water bottle. Then she sat back down and played with the bottle.

Finally, her parents arrived. They wouldn't hear anything of her driving her car.

"I'll drive it," Dad insisted.

She held up the empty water bottle. "I'm hydrated now. Perfectly capable. Everyone made too big of a deal over the whole thing."

Mom kissed her cheek. "It's our job to be concerned."

"You're doing phenomenally well."

On the way home, Dad gave her the third degree.

She stuffed her hands in her pockets so he wouldn't see them shaking. What if they figured out she was pregnant? Would they ground her? Make her get rid of it? Could they even do that?

"Are you sure you aren't on one of those diets?" he asked.

"Would you stop? I'm eating plenty. I just didn't have enough water today, which is always a bad idea when I have PE."

He glanced over at her. "You're sure that's all it is?"

"What else would it be? I'm not dieting, even though everyone seems to think I am."

"We just care, Hadley."

She sighed dramatically, hoping he'd figure out how much they were all annoying her.

"What do we need to do to make sure you drink enough water from now on?"

"I'll drink more water."

"That isn't a plan. Should we stock up your locker with water bottles?"

"No. I'll drink from every fountain I see, all day long. Every time I see a fountain, that'll be my reminder. Problem solved."

"Are you sure? We can't have a repeat of this."

"We *won't*. I'm fine."

He pulled up to the curb and parked her car. She grabbed the keys and hurried up to her room. All anyone wanted was for her to rest, and that gave her the perfect excuse to hide in her room all afternoon.

But hiding out was the last thing her parents would let her do. Every five seconds, one of them knocked on her door to check on her. They even sent Grandma, Zeke, and Luna to mix things up.

The third time Dad knocked, she glared at him. "If you guys don't leave me alone to study, I'm going to the library."

"You have to stay home."

"No, I need to get my English project done."

He sat next to her on the bed.

"This is the opposite of leaving me alone."

"Is there anything you aren't telling us?"

Her heart thundered so loud she was sure he could hear.

She cleared her throat. "No. Why do you ask?"

"You fainted today."

"I didn't pass out. Just dizzy."

"Either way, that isn't normal."

"You don't think so? Given all the stress I'm under? First, my boyfriend dies, then everyone thought you killed him, Grandma is getting frail, and now Wes has threatened me. I think I'm handling everything quite well considering!"

Dad frowned. "Are you worried about Wes?"

She shrugged. Not that she was going to tell him that the knife in her pocket eased her worries.

"Did he say anything else? Something you didn't tell us?"

"No."

The lines around his eyes became more pronounced and he leaped to his feet. "That's it. I'm going to have some words with him. This has to stop."

"Wait, Dad—"

He marched to her door, only turning around before closing the door. "You stay here. I'm going to make sure he doesn't bother you again."

With that, he slammed the door.

Chapter Twenty-One

BRAD BARELY ACKNOWLEDGED the greetings from neighbors as he stormed to the Campbells' house. He should've dealt with this as soon as Hadley told them about Wes's threat. Faye had wanted him to have some time to think and calm down, and look where that had gotten them — their daughter had passed out at school from the stress of it.

It ended now.

He was in luck. Wes stood trimming some hedges in his yard, his back to Brad. He couldn't hide and pretend he wasn't home. There would also be witnesses if he tried to assault him.

Brad clenched his fists as he made his way to the other man.

Wes was so into the job at hand, he didn't hear Brad's approach.

The trimmers were so loud with their constant *clip, clip, clip*.

Clip, clip, clip, squeak.

Brad hesitated, debating whether he should wait for

Wes to turn around and surprise him then, or if he should announce his presence now.

Clip, clip, clip.

The sound was grating. Making his heart pound harder than it already was.

Clip, squeak.

Wes lowered the tool and examined it.

The sweet silence rang in Brad's ears. "Wes."

He jumped and nearly dropped the trimmers. Slowly turned around, his brows furrowed. "What are you doing on my property?"

"I'm here to ask why you threatened my teenage daughter."

"Threatened?"

"You told her she'd be sorry, Wes. Why did you say that?"

He held the blades up in front of his chest and stared at Brad. The blades were a cobalt blue — faded by years of clipping branches. But they were blue nonetheless.

BlueBlade clippers, a summer line that had been discontinued years earlier.

Wes snapped the blades open and shut. "She's pestering my son. I told her to stay away from my family. I meant it, and needed to make myself clear."

Brad took a step closer, his anger building. He took measured breaths through his nose to keep from showing any emotion. "Don't ever poke my daughter again."

"If she stays away from my family, that won't be a problem."

"Whether or not she does is irrelevant." From the corner of his vision, a few neighbors gathered. Brad raised his voice. "Do not touch my daughter again. Or any member of my family, myself included."

Wes snapped the clippers open and closed. "You need to get off my property."

"Have I made myself clear?"

"Crystal. If you ever step foot on my property again, I'm calling the cops."

"Be sure to mention your infidelities when you do. That's vital information regarding Allison's case."

Wes's mouth gaped slightly and his eyes narrowed. "I said, leave."

"Gladly. And anything you do to my daughter, I will return to you tenfold." Brad backed up, keeping his focus on the blades until he reached the sidewalk. "Stay away from Hadley!"

The neighbors whispered among themselves.

Good. Let them draw whatever conclusions they wanted. Wes needed to know he wasn't untouchable. Now people would be watching him even closer.

Brad's only regret was that he hadn't gotten the chance to say more before getting kicked off the property. But it was fine. He'd said plenty, and the neighbors had heard — hopefully *enough* to question him. To apply necessary heat. They would wonder about the circumstances in which Wes had touched a teenager.

But now there was no question. Wes knew there would be consequences if he went anywhere near Hadley again.

This was Brad's last warning. He was done playing the nice guy.

He reached for his phone to call Faye, but realized he'd left it at the house.

At home, he found it sitting on the bed. Must have fallen out of his pocket earlier when discussing Hadley's health with Faye. He checked for messages.

Kurt had called several times.

Brad's stomach knotted. What was going on now?

He locked himself in his office before calling his boss back.

"Where have you been?" Kurt answered.

"Dealing with neighborhood stuff. What's going on?"

"I haven't heard from you. Was worried something had gone wrong. Everything okay?"

"One of my kids is having health issues, but I think it's just stress — and that's been dealt with."

"Good." Kurt sounded relieved. "Is there anything you need from me?"

"No."

"Are you sure? I'm here if you do."

Brad collapsed onto his chair. "I appreciate it. But everything seems to be coming together with my family."

"Does that mean your mother is improving?"

"She's doing great, and I can't see signs of mental deterioration like the doctor mentioned."

"That's great news." Kurt cleared his throat. "I hate to bring this up, but are you working on your target? Time is ticking, and my intel says it's only a matter of time before he moves. Last time, he was off the radar for years. We can't afford that."

Brad rubbed his temples. "I'm on it."

"When?"

"Tonight." The word flew from his mouth before he'd had time to think.

"Tonight?" Kurt's smile could be heard through the phone. "You're superman. Not that I ever doubted you."

Meaning others had, and voiced their concerns to Kurt.

"I can balance work and family, even with so much going on. Like I said, tonight's my night."

"That's fantastic. Really. Are you going to his house?"

"As a last resort. There's that cabin he goes to every weeknight. It's the perfect location. No witnesses."

"And it'll lead the cops to the evidence they were too blind to locate before."

"Exactly."

"Check in after the deed is done. Dad's breathing down my neck about this one."

"Will do." Brad ended the call and closed his eyes, every muscle in his body aching. The only thing he wanted after the last few days was to sit with a cold beer and decompress.

That would have to wait until he took care of his target.

He looked over the file and the notes he'd taken. Belsky should be at his cabin in just under three hours. That would give Brad just enough time to stake the place out before taking the lowlife down.

But first he would have to break the news to Faye that he wouldn't be home for the rest of the evening. She would have to watch his mom and the kids all night.

He was going to owe her.

After gathering his things, he found Faye in the kitchen with his mother.

She dropped what she was doing and hurried over to him. "Where are you going?"

He pulled her into the hall. "I have to go to work."

Faye glanced at his bag. "You mean ... you have a ... a *job*?"

"Right."

Color drained from her face. "You're going to kill someone?"

"Someone who's been trafficking girls younger than Hadley. I'm saving lives."

She leaned against the wall and closed her eyes.

He put his hand on her shoulder. "I know I'm leaving you with a lot to deal with tonight with the kids, my mom, Bingo—"

"It isn't that." She opened her eyes. "I can deal with that, obviously. I just … how am I supposed to go along and act like everything is normal when I know you're going to be taking a life?"

"Think of all the girls I'm saving. More than likely, he has several in his cabin right now. They'll be rescued before being sold to someone else."

She didn't look convinced.

"He needs to be taken down before he can hurt anyone else."

"What about the justice system? He should be tried and put in prison."

"They can't even catch him."

Faye's eyes lit up. "You should quit!"

"What?"

"Yeah. There's so many other things you could do."

"In this town?"

"Why not?"

Brad drew a deep breath. He didn't want to tell her there was no quitting this business — not if he wanted to keep his life. "My job is necessary for the safety of society. How many times do we have to go over this?"

"It doesn't feel right."

"To save innocent girls?"

Faye frowned. "That part does."

"Then focus on that." He kissed her. "I'm saving not only those girls, but countless others in the future. The police can't do it, so I am. Nobody will ever know what I did, but I don't need the recognition. Rest assured that those girls will have a new chance at life. That's making a difference in the world."

"I can't deny that." She sighed.

He pulled her into his arms. "The world will be safer place when I return home. But I need to get going or I'm going to run into trouble."

Her eyes widened. "Meaning?"

"I'll lose the element of surprise." He brushed his lips across hers. "Don't worry about me."

Fear shone in her eyes. "How can I not?"

"Because coming home to you and the kids is what gets me through each of my jobs."

Chapter Twenty-Two

SNAP!

Brad jolted to attention. Pushed aside the bush for a better view. That snapping branch had to be Belsky. Nobody else would be out this far into the woods, so close to the cabin, and not many forest animals would be large enough to make loud of a noise.

He held his breath. Double-checked his rifle. In position. Ready to fire.

Waited.

Nothing but silence.

He hadn't made a sound, so what was the hold up? The noise had come from the right direction. It had to be his man. Or a bear. Either way, he was ready.

Snap!

Brad glanced over through the rifle's viewer.

It was him. The idiot was whistling a tune as he was coming to his hidden house of horrors. Not that he was the one on the receiving end of any of it.

Brad readjusted the gun's position slightly, watching.

Belsky had a girl with him. This made it slightly more tricky.

Only slightly. Brad knew what he was doing. This would be quick, and the girl would likely run off. He couldn't get involved even if he wanted to — it would put the whole company in danger of being discovered by law enforcement. They *had* to stay undercover.

Belsky moved behind the girl.

Now it was more complicated. Brad could still go for the man's head. A fatal shot, sure. But he preferred the chest. More wiggle room. But he could still do this.

He would.

Breath hitched, he readjusted his aim. Held the trigger.

Waited.

Pulled it.

Again.

Bang! Bang!

Brad readied himself for a possible third shot.

His target went down.

The girl screamed. Turned in circles. Yelled again.

"Run," Brad muttered.

She pulled at her ratty hair, stared down at her captor. Hollered again.

He rang out another shot far from her.

The girl took the clue and bolted.

Brad breathed a sigh of relief, stood, and dusted himself off. Just needed to check that Belsky was dead, then he could start the long drive back home.

That had been one of his easier missions. And that was exactly why he preferred kills like this out in the middle of nowhere. Not the losers like the one he'd had to follow into a store and then a parking lot. What a nightmare — and of course that'd been the one time he'd been jumped during a hit.

Brad rubbed his ears to help the ringing go down and listened to make sure the girl wasn't heading back this way. The sound of the leaves rustling was getting softer.

He made sure the rifle was ready in case he came across a wild animal and went around the bush to check the man on the ground.

A pool of blood encircled his head. Two shots on his forehead right next to each other.

He wouldn't be hurting anyone again.

Once in civilization, Brad would find a pay phone — those still existed in rural places near the woods like this — and drop a clue to the local authorities about the girl and the cabin. They would figure out the rest.

He started down the same path his target had taken and thought about picking up a dessert for Faye.

Something struck his shoulder.

He lost his balance.

His grip on the rifle loosened. He managed to keep hold of it.

Something shoved him. No, someone.

They both tumbled to the ground.

Brad's rifle went flying. He swore. Pushed the other man. Couldn't see his face. A mask.

Belsky was supposed to be working alone. Had that changed? It couldn't have. Brad had done his homework. He would have known if the man had been working with someone.

Yet here he was wrestling on the forest floor with someone equally as tall and muscular as Brad.

Someone who was here for Brad personally. It was the only explanation.

He was being targeted again.

At least this time it was only one attacker.

So far.

Brad hit, kicked, and wrestled, trying to get the man's mask off.

The other man punched his chest, momentarily knocking the air from his lungs. He struck Brad's cheek. Pain swelled under his eye.

Adrenaline took over, and Brad fought back, managing to pin his attacker to the ground before he'd fully gotten his breath back.

He ripped off the mask. Even in the small bit of moonlight filtering to the path, Brad could tell he didn't know him. "Who are you?"

The man struggled, but didn't say anything.

Brad dug his knee into his neck. "I said, who are you?"

He spat on him.

Brad whipped out a knife and pressed it to his attacker's throat. "Talk, if you want a chance of seeing tomorrow."

"Not telling you nothin'."

Brad pressed the blade into his skin, drawing blood. "Sure about that?"

His only response was to squirm.

"If that's the way you want to have it." Brad shoved the knife farther in.

"Stop!"

Brad pulled the blade back a little. "Yes?"

"What do you want to know?"

"Who you're working for! Why you're trying to kill me."

"Campbell." The man coughed, squirmed.

"Campbell?" Brad nearly dropped his weapon. "You can't mean Wes."

"Yes, him." He coughed again, this time yanking one arm free and putting pressure on his wound. "He wants you dead."

"Why are you giving him up so easily?"

"Easily? You'll kill me otherwise."

"How did Wes know where I'd be?" Brad demanded. "Or did you follow me? But that's impossible. I checked. Took an unusual route."

"Can I sit up?"

Brad studied the guy. Couldn't be more than thirty. Practically a kid. He slid off him but pressed the blade to him. "How did Wes know where I'd be?"

"I don't know. He just gave me the coordinates and your picture."

Anger pulsated through his body. "That's impossible."

The guy coughed again. "I just needed the money. That's all I know — I swear."

"Wes Campbell? Married to Allison? Three kids?"

"Yeah. I don't know about the kids, though. His wife is dead, and he's glad. She was getting too close to the truth."

"What truth?"

"I don't *know*, man. Everything is above my pay grade."

"Yet he sent you to take *me* out?"

"Yeah." He rubbed his neck. "You got a Band-Aid or something?"

"No, I don't have a Band-Aid." Brad shook his head in disbelief. "Have you even killed anyone before?"

"Yeah."

"A trained assassin?"

He shook his head.

"That much is obvious. Wes is an idiot for sending you."

The guy scooted back.

Brad grabbed his arm and squeezed. "Tell me everything you know about Wes. Who does *he* work for?"

"I told you. I don't know nothin'. I'm not even working for the company. Just him."

"Company? What company?" Brad applied more pressure.

"The car wash place."

"Which one?" Brad's voice was near a yell.

"The Slippery Fish car wash."

Brad's thoughts swirled around like a raging river. Did Wes work for a similar organization? Or did he just think he was a big-time boss in a small town? And why such a lame cover? But then again, nobody would ever suspect criminal activity from a place called the Slippery Fish.

On the other hand, what if there *was* a similar assassin business in town? Was Kurt aware of it?

Could more of his neighbors be involved?

How deep did this go?

"Can I go now?"

"No." Brad turned to him. "You can thank Wes for that."

"Wait, what?"

Brad raised the knife and aimed it for the guy's chest.

Chapter Twenty-Three

HADLEY WAVED to Ellie and Lucy before heading to the bathroom. It was the fourth time today, and it was only lunch. At least she was staying hydrated. She hadn't been the slightest bit dizzy, much less fallen over or seen those dancing dots.

She was right and everyone else was wrong. It had only been a hydration issue.

When she entered the bathroom, the overwhelming smells of perfumes and hairspray nearly gagged her. A group of four cheerleaders were giggling.

They stopped as soon as they saw her.

"You don't have to stop having fun on my account."

The girls just stared at Hadley until she closed the stall door between them.

No way she could pee now. The silence rang out like a loudspeaker. Everyone would hear her.

She waited. They neither left nor carried on with their conversation.

This was awesome. It was so obvious she wasn't doing anything in there.

"What are you waiting for?" asked one of the girls. It sounded like Violet or maybe Daphne. They both basically sounded the same.

"Yeah, really." That was definitely Norah. Her voice was so high-pitched it could break glass. "One of the teachers?"

"Like Mr. Beasley?" Shay asked. "He's pretty hot. Not like Duke Hill, but smokin' in his own way. Know what I mean?"

Hadley nearly dropped her bag. Caught it.

Those airheads couldn't know about Duke.

They couldn't.

But why else would Shay mention him?

"Cat got your tongue?" Violet-or-Daphne laughed.

"Or maybe Mr. Beasley isn't old enough for her?"

Laughter filled the bathroom.

Hadley burst out of the stall. "What are you losers talking about?"

Daphne raked her fingers through her bleach-blonde hair. "Duke Hill."

"Why?"

Shay squared her shoulders. "Why don't *you* tell us."

Heat crept into Hadley's cheeks. "He's dead. What is there to laugh about?"

"Other than the fact that you two were doing the nasty?"

Hadley's mouth fell open.

Violet stepped closer to her. "Was he nailing you when he got killed?"

They all burst into laughter.

Norah smirked. "He was one hill I would have gladly climbed. Too bad I never got the chance. He'd have never looked at you again after seeing what I can do."

Everything took on a red hue.

Hadley dropped her bag and lunged for Norah, swinging her fists wildly.

Violet and Daphne shoved her out of the way.

"Watch it." Norah glowered at her. "You'll regret laying a hand on me. My dad's a lawyer, don't forget."

"And yours is a killer." Shay smirked.

They all laughed again.

Hadley shirked away from Violet and Daphne. "Don't talk bad about Duke *or* my dad!"

"Why not?" Norah pursed her lips. "One was a cradle robber and the other is a cold-hearted killer. That's why Duke is dead, isn't it? I'd think you'd want your daddy punished for killing your boyfriend."

Hadley punched her in the face. "Shut up! If you ever say anything about them again, you won't be able to run home to your daddy or tell him what I did. Got it?"

Norah covered her face. "I can't believe you just hit me!"

"Leave me alone!" Hadley barely remembered to grab her bag before storming out of the bathroom. She still had to pee, but she couldn't face those four again.

She ran down the hall, turning away from her next class.

Tears stung her eyes, and she blinked them away.

How could those four know about Duke?

Nate.

She never should have trusted him. But he'd had those sad puppy-dog eyes because of his dead mom. Made her think they had something in common because they'd both lost someone.

They had nothing in common. He was just like his dad. Vindictive and mean.

Why had she thought they could be friends? She should've opened up to Ellie and Lucy, not him.

Now the whole school would know about her and Duke.

If they didn't already.

She nearly crashed into someone.

Ellie.

Her best friend stared at her with distrust. "Is it true?"

"What?" Hadley's stomach knotted.

Ellie had heard through the rumor mill. Hadley should've told her herself. Or better yet, never spilled her secret to Nate.

"Don't play dumb with me." Ellie's eyebrows furrowed. "You *were* seeing Duke Hill. That explains everything. Why you stopped hanging out with us, why you've been so depressed since he died. I chalked it up to you being stressed about your dad being the main suspect."

Hadley looked away. "I wanted to tell you."

"No, you didn't."

"I did."

"You've had all this time, and you haven't said one word. Nothing! And I thought we were best friends."

Tears blurred Hadley's vision. She let them fall. "We are. I couldn't tell anyone about Duke. He could've gotten into trouble because I wasn't eighteen yet."

"You could've told me. I wouldn't have blabbed your secret."

Hadley wiped her face. "I know, but I promised him."

The hurt in Ellie's eyes crushed Hadley.

"I wanted to tell you." Her words barely came out above a whisper.

"You should've."

"I know."

Ellie crossed her arms. "What about Nate?"

"What about him?"

"You had no problem telling *him*."

More tears ran down Hadley's face, tickling as they trailed down. "It came out accidentally when he was talking about his mom's death. I didn't mean to tell him."

"But you did."

Hadley looked away again and wiped her tears, but it was pointless. They were falling too fast.

"I can't believe you'd do this to me. Do you know who told me?"

"No."

"Lizzie McGowan of all people! *She* knew, and I didn't — your lifelong best friend. But that was all a lie, wasn't it?"

"It wasn't!" Hadley reached for Ellie.

She stepped away, tears shining in her eyes. "Don't touch me!"

Hadley choked back a sob. "Ellie."

Her best friend shook her head and ran down the hall.

Hadley wanted to race after her, but had no energy. And it wasn't like Ellie would hear her out.

Besides, she needed to get to the bathroom before she peed her pants.

She ran down the hallway. Some basketball players called out derogatory names, pointing to her and laughing.

Hadley raced into the nearest bathroom. Thankfully, it was empty. She scurried into the nearest stall and released the floodgates. The tears still hadn't stopped.

Now the whole school knew about her and Duke, and her best friend wanted nothing to do with her. And her hand hurt from hitting Norah's hard head. If her dad really was a lawyer, she was probably going to get in serious trouble for that. Not to mention the school's no-violence policy.

She covered her mouth and sobbed, shaking so hard it made her stomach lurch.

This wasn't the way her junior year was supposed to go. Her plan had been to win all kinds of academic and athletic awards, and enjoy life.

Everyone said these were her best years.

But how could it get worse?

She blew her nose, then stood to flush.

Stopped cold.

The toilet water was bright red.

Chapter Twenty-Four

Faye closed the front door and leaned against it, every bone in her body aching. She'd had three grouchy clients in a row, and the last one had hated her haircut. Faye had made it look exactly like the picture, but it had been a drastic change — more than the client had anticipated, and she took her frustrations out on Faye. Both verbally and by withholding the tip.

She couldn't wait to open her own salon and not rely on the tips. Simply charging for the cuts would be a huge pay raise. If she could get Luna to bed early, she would work on her plans for the salon.

At least Brad was finally on board. That was ninety percent of the battle. Now it was a matter of turning their junk room into her business. And even better than that, she would be able to stay home with Dianne if she would be staying with them long-term.

Things were finally looking up.

If only she could get past Brad's real job. She'd been a nervous wreck the entire time he'd been gone the night before. But he returned clean and smiling, with a caramel cheesecake in hand. There was a faint mark under one eye, but she hadn't been able to bring herself to ask about it. Wasn't sure she really wanted to know how it got there.

It was almost as if he had simply been at BlueBlade all evening. Maybe that was what she needed to tell herself to get through his hits. Just another night at the office.

Except that normal jobs didn't put people's lives in danger like that.

"Mom?" Hadley called. "Is that you?"

"Right here, honey." Faye locked the deadbolt, kicked off her shoes, and headed upstairs.

Hadley stood outside her bedroom door, face drained of color.

Faye dropped her purse and raced over. "Did you faint again?"

"No." Hadley wiped her eyes. They were red like she'd been crying.

"What's the matter?"

Hadley held her gaze, her stare intense. "I have to tell you something."

Faye's breath hitched. "What?"

"In here." Hadley dragged her into the bedroom and locked the door. "I've been keeping a secret."

That was barely a surprise after the whole Duke thing. Though that didn't keep her throat from drying. She looked expectantly at her daughter.

Hadley chewed on her lower lip and played with her hair.

Faye struggled to keep her composure. One wrong move, and Hadley could decide to keep her secret to herself. "What, sweetie? You can tell me anything."

"I'm pregnant."

The words stung. Rang in her ears. She had to have heard wrong. "Pregnant?"

Hadley nodded. "I don't know what happened."

"I think we both know what happened."

"What I mean is that Duke was really careful."

Faye didn't want to hear the details, but needed to keep her daughter talking. "Nothing is one hundred percent effective. But are you sure?"

Hadley opened a drawer of her nightstand and pulled out three pregnancy tests. They were all positive.

Faye covered her mouth. The reality of the situation hit her like a gale-force wind. Her baby was going to have a baby. Except that she didn't have to. There were ways to fix situations like this. "Do you need me to make an appointment for you?"

"I think so. I've been bleeding, and it won't stop."

Faye's stomach dropped. "When did this start? How much? Is that why you passed out?"

"One question at a time, Mom. No, this isn't why I *almost* fainted. I was dehydrated, like I told you. This started today, at school."

"And you didn't think to tell anyone sooner?"

"I was dealing with some stuff at school that was stressing me out. I looked it up online, and stress can cause bleeding. But it isn't supposed to keep going like it is. I think something might be wrong with the baby."

Faye buried her face in her palms.

"I should also probably tell you that the whole school knows about me and Duke."

"What?" Faye's heart pounded like a jackhammer. People would draw conclusions that Brad killed Duke.

This was what he'd feared all along.

Hadley sniffled. "I hope this doesn't make things bad for Dad."

Faye embraced her. "Rose is already charged for that. It's better now than before."

"There's something else."

"More?" Faye tensed.

"I punched a loudmouth cheerleader. Her dad's a lawyer."

"What did you do that for?"

"She was talking crap about both Dad and Duke. Everyone was laughing at me. What else was I supposed to do?"

"Walk away."

Hadley scowled. "Easier said than done."

"That's why it's called taking the high road."

"Look, I'm just trying to get your help. If you want, I can find it somewhere else."

Faye imagined her finding someone older and more dangerous than Duke. "And I want to help you, but you need to understand that I'm going to react to you telling me some things."

"It's only natural, I guess."

"Thank you."

"Just like me punching Norah."

"Hardly. You could've walked away, and I'm not hitting anyone. Now let's get back to your health. How much are you bleeding?"

Hadley shrugged. "I went through a pad." She shuddered. "I hate those things, but I didn't think anything else would be good at this point."

"You haven't had any prenatal care. Right?"

She shook her head. "But I bought some prenatal vitamins and have been taking those."

"There's a lot more to taking care of yourself when pregnant than that. We need to get you to a doctor right now." Faye wrung her hands together, trying not to think of all the things that could go wrong.

"Do we have to tell Dad?"

"You'd better believe it."

"Can't we wait?"

"He's your father. He needs to know what's going on."

Tears shone in her eyes. "Please, Mom. He's going to flip."

"Maybe you should've thought of that before you got yourself into this mess. Speaking of that — how far along are you?"

Hadley shrugged again.

"You don't know when this happened?"

"Obviously before he died," she snapped.

"And you're sure it's Duke's?"

"Get out!" Hadley leaped up, then grabbed her abdomen. "Just go! I never should've said anything to you. I'll take care of this myself."

"No, you won't."

"How could you ask such a question? Of course it's his! Who else's would it be?"

"I don't know you as well as I thought I did, so I have to ask these things."

Hadley crossed her arms, and a tear trailed down her face. "I never want another boyfriend ever again. It's his."

She would change her mind about having other boyfriends, but Faye managed to keep her thoughts to herself. "Understood. We need to talk to your dad and get you to a doctor." She glanced at the time. "Probably Urgent Care at this point."

Hadley frowned, but at least didn't put up a fuss.

Faye looked out into the hall, not seeing Brad. She didn't dare leave Hadley alone in her room. Who knew what she'd do? She seemed to live for making one bad decision after another these days. "Let's find him."

"You want me to come with you? I thought I was supposed to rest."

"I'm not letting you out of my sight."

Hadley glared at her.

"Not helping your cause. Come on."

With her daughter trailing behind, Faye looked in her bedroom. Brad wasn't there.

She knocked on his office door.

"I'm busy!"

"This is important."

"Life or death?"

"Yes!"

A moment later, the door opened and Brad appeared. "What's wrong?"

Faye glanced at Hadley. "Your daughter has something to tell you."

"My daughter? This doesn't sound good."

"Mom." Hadley pleaded with her eyes.

"You got yourself into this very adult situation."

"*Please.*" Tears ran down her face.

Color drained from Brad's face. "What the hell is going on?"

Hadley grabbed Faye's arms. "Mom!"

Faye turned to Brad. "She's pregnant. We have to get her to a doctor because she's bleeding."

The range of emotions on Brad's face would have been comical under any other circumstances. At that moment, it took all of Faye's self-control to keep from dissolving into tears herself.

A gasp sounded behind them.

Zeke stood there, his eyes wide and his hands over his mouth.

Hadley spun around and limped to her room, her hands on her stomach, and slammed the door.

Faye whipped around and narrowed her eyes at Zeke. "This is family business. You don't tell *anyone* else. Got it?"

He nodded, still wide-eyed.

"Is it Duke's?"

"Go to your room!" Faye pointed to it.

He stormed inside and slammed his door.

Brad turned to her. "*Is* it Duke's?"

She nodded. "We need to get her seen now."

"I'll call—"

Thud! Thump! Whack! Thud! Thud!

Faye and Brad both turned to the stairs where the noise was coming from. Without a word, they both raced over.

Dianne lay at the bottom, motionless.

Chapter Twenty-Five

BRAD GLANCED AT THE TIME. Again. Checked his phone. Still nothing from Faye. She was waiting for Hadley, who was being seen at the maternity care area while Brad waited for news on his mom's surgery. All he knew was they were lucky she'd survived the tumble down the stairs — not that he needed a doctor to tell him that much. And he was still trying to wrap his head around Hadley's pregnancy. Why hadn't she taken care of that already? Kids didn't need their parents' permission for that stuff anymore.

He was also waiting to hear back from Kurt, who had turned elusive again. His boss had been so eager for Brad to make his kill but then ghosted him when Brad tried to discuss what had happened.

With Wes involved in the hit on Brad, there were now more questions. At least he knew who really killed Allison — not that it had ever been that big of a question. Just a matter of getting the police to see it. If they didn't, Wes would eventually end up on BlueBlade's radar. Although, if

Brad's attacker was right, there was another assassin business in town.

And that seemed unlikely. How could that go unnoticed by Kurt and Ralf? Kurt's dad had been in the business for at least fifty years. Nothing went undetected by him. He was the all-knowing, elusive leader of everything in BlueBlade.

The attacker had to be lying. Or Wes lied to him. But the fact that he'd been attacked twice on hits showed he wasn't playing with an amateur.

Wes Campbell knew what he was doing. He probably even had something to do with Duke's murder. In fact, given how well he and Rose had taken to each other, it made sense that they had started working together before they supposedly met at Brad's Super Bowl party.

The whole scenario continued to grow deeper and more complicated with every new piece of information. And that was exactly why he needed to speak with Kurt.

The fact that he couldn't reach his boss again after being attacked made it hard for him to trust the man. He was Brad's best friend one day and then untouchable the next.

It sure made him look guilty of something. Or suspicious at the very least.

Brad checked his phone again and sent another text to both his wife and his boss. Hopefully, one of them would get back to him soon.

When he didn't get a response, his mind wandered back to Rose and Wes. She had to have been the person he'd been seeing behind Allison's back. Did she pull Wes into the business and make him think the car wash was the assassin front? At least she'd been smart enough to keep BlueBlade out of it.

Brad couldn't sit still another moment. He stuffed his

phone in his pocket and wandered around the waiting room, looking at the fish tanks. It just made him think of the Slippery Fish car wash.

He went over to the desk and asked about his mom.

The nurse typed on his computer. "Looks like she's in surgery."

"Surgery? Why didn't the doctor talk to me?"

"It's busy tonight, and we're short on staff. Five people out with a stomach flu."

Brad bit back an irritated comment. "You have my number, right?"

The nurse glanced at the screen and read off the digits.

"Have the doctor call me as soon as she can. I'm going to check on someone who's in another part of the hospital."

"Will do." He turned to the person next in line.

Brad checked his phone, finding no new texts as expected. Just as he reached the maternity waiting room, a text came in from Faye.

He found her. "My mom's in surgery. What's going on with Hadley? Is she okay?"

"Is your mom going to be okay?"

"Yes, but I'm still waiting to hear more from the doctor. They're understaffed and don't have time for me."

She frowned. "Hadley's almost ready to be released. She's hooked up to an IV for fluids and they want to observe her for another hour. If all goes well, she can come home. But she has to rest for a few days. No school, or online only for the rest of the week. And she has to limit her activities."

"You make it sound like she's keeping it."

"The doctor said she won't discuss terminating. He wants us to talk her into it, but in the meantime is starting her on prenatal care."

Brad collapsed onto the chair. "I can't believe this is happening. Doesn't she know what this will do to her future?"

Faye sighed. "She sees it as her only link to Duke."

"What about the love letters? The sweatshirt? All those pictures she keeps scrolling through?"

"She told me it would be like killing him all over again."

"He's already dead!"

"I know, but her first love was murdered, plus she's young and hormonal. Logic isn't flying at the moment. The more anyone pushes, the harder she digs her heels in."

"We need to make her. We're still legally responsible for her."

"Not medically — not since she turned thirteen."

"But we're in charge of paying for her medical bills."

Faye nodded.

"This is so backwards."

"With any luck, this trip to the hospital will be a wakeup call."

"Especially when I present her with the bill," he muttered.

Brad's phone buzzed. He pulled it out of his pocket. A text from the ER.

"What is it?" Faye asked.

"The doctor wants to talk to me. Let me know when Hadley's released."

She nodded.

They embraced before he responded to the text, letting them know he'd be right there. Then he rushed back to the ER before the doctor got too busy to speak with him again.

Thankfully, she was still in the waiting room talking with another family. Once she was done with them, she turned to Brad. Most of what she said went over his head, but from what he gathered, his mom was expected to make a full recovery.

"You're welcome to stay and wait, but the operation could last a few more hours. I'd suggest going home for some rest so you can visit in the morning."

"Visit?"

"She's going to have to stay for observation. If all goes well, she could be released tomorrow afternoon, but it could well go longer. It's too soon to say for certain."

"You'll call me as soon as she's out of surgery?"

The doctor nodded. "I'll update you, yes. But there's one more thing we need to discuss."

Brad's stomach knotted. "What?"

"You'll need to find a way to keep her away from the stairs. It's too dangerous."

"Sure, okay."

"Do you have a plan?"

"A plan?"

"We can't release her unless you have a plan to keep her from going on any stairs."

Brad closed his eyes for a moment. "We have some baby gates in the garage. I'll put those up."

"Good. And her bedroom isn't upstairs?"

He hadn't thought of the guest room. They had no bedrooms downstairs.

"If you don't, you'll have to figure out where she will sleep. Like I said, you need a plan."

"We have a room she can use." They would have to convert their junk room into his mom's room.

That meant Faye wouldn't be able to build her in-home salon.

And he was going to have to be the one to break it to her.

Chapter Twenty-Six

BRAD PACED outside Kurt's office. He was in there, and he had to come out sometime. Brad would wait all day if necessary. All night. Bust the door down if he had to.

The door to the shop opened and Justin came in. "Having fun?"

Brad ignored him and tried to burn holes in the door with his gaze.

"How's the website coming?" Justin asked.

"What's your problem?" Brad snapped.

"Nothing. What's yours?"

"Waiting for Kurt."

"Have fun with that." Justin pulled out a sack lunch from his locker and sat at the table.

Great. He wasn't going anywhere.

"The website doesn't look any different to me. Why are you really working from home?"

"Would you shut it?" Brad glowered at him.

Justin muttered, and turned his back to Brad.

Finally, peace.

Brad texted Kurt again to remind him he was waiting

out there. Checked for any new texts from Faye or the hospital. Nothing.

Last night, he and Faye barely had time to say goodnight to each other before going to bed. He still needed to give her the bad news about the spare room downstairs.

She'd insisted on sleeping in Hadley's room the previous night. Hadley hadn't been thrilled, but was too tired to put up much of a fuss. Brad was relieved that Faye was in there with her, though he'd missed having her with him. It would've been the perfect night to talk into the wee hours. But it was for the best. Their daughter needed her more, and hopefully she'd be rested by the time they spoke about the home salon. She'd still been asleep when he'd left after making sure Zeke and Luna got on their buses. They'd both eaten donuts for breakfast — something Faye wouldn't have approved of — but they were dressed and fed. He'd done his job.

Kurt's doorknob jiggled.

Brad stopped in his tracks. Was his boss actually going to talk to him now?

A tall, thick guy with salt-and-pepper hair and an expensive suit stepped out, his expression grim. He glared at Brad before storming out the back door.

Just before Kurt's office door closed, Brad stuck his foot in the way to block it. Stepped inside and closed it behind him.

His boss looked up and sighed.

"Avoiding me?"

"You saw that guy?" Kurt said.

"Mr. Friendly?"

"Yeah, him. He's my problem right now. Can't think about anything else."

"Well, you're going to have to because you won't believe what I'm about to tell you."

Kurt rubbed his eyes. "You were jumped. You already told me in your numerous messages."

"Two times in as many months!"

"Why is that?" Kurt's expression stiffened. "Should I be concerned about your performance?"

"What? No. What we need to talk about isn't the fact that I was attacked again."

"You killed the guy. Obviously, he won't be a problem from here on out."

"Would you let me finish?" Brad threw his hands in the air. "He told me some concerning information before he died."

Kurt tilted his head, and motioned for Brad to sit across from him.

At last.

Brad plopped down.

"What did he say?" The lines around his eyes and on his forehead deepened.

"We aren't the only assassin business in town."

Kurt didn't blink. "Excuse me?"

"I think he might've been mistaken — lied to, really. But I can't ignore what was said."

"Tell me everything." Kurt's mouth formed a straight line, his pupils dilated.

"It's complicated, and I've been trying to connect all the dots, but it—"

"What did he *say*?" Kurt slammed his fist on the desk.

Brad hesitated. "That he was working for Wes Campbell, and that his company was through the Slippery Fish."

"He told you that?"

"Yes."

"He was making that up to keep you from killing him."

Brad studied him. "Are you sure?"

"I know *everything* that goes on in this town. You think I

194

wouldn't know about another undercover operation? There wouldn't be room for two."

"But he—"

"Rose got close to your neighbor. She probably made up the car wash thing to cover for BlueBlade. And now Campbell thinks he's some big shot and is shooting off his mouth and trying to make you pay for getting his lover arrested. And you fell for it, hook, line, and sinker."

Brad stared at him in disbelief. "You won't even look into it?"

"The man obviously killed his wife and he's distraught about his girlfriend being in the slammer. You're getting too close, so he hired someone to scare you."

"But he knew where I went to kill my target! I was in the middle of nowhere."

Kurt shrugged. "Maybe you weren't being careful. Wouldn't surprise me. Brad, I'm more than happy to help you, but you have to drop this theory. You're stretched too thin between your mom and daughter. Stop making things up about things you know nothing about."

Brad's blood ran cold. Now Kurt knew about Hadley? "How closely are you following me?"

"I'm going to say this exactly one time. Focus on your family. Take whatever time you need. Don't worry about anything unless I tell you to. Understood?"

He nodded.

The last thing he was going to do was stop looking into Wes or the Slippery Fish.

Chapter Twenty-Seven

FAYE ADDED a note to her salon blueprints when the front door slammed shut.

"Are you here, Faye?" Brad called.

"In the kitchen." She added another note to the drawing.

He appeared in the doorway and leaned against it. "We have to talk."

Faye's stomach knotted at his tone. "It isn't your mom, is it?"

"It has to do with her."

She studied him, trying to figure out what he was getting at.

Brad sat next to her and took her hand.

"This can't be good."

"The doctor said the only way she can release my mom into our care is if we have a plan to keep her away from the stairs."

Faye blinked a few times, trying to connect the dots. "Okay. But why are you acting like something's wrong? We can figure something out."

He hesitated. "There isn't an easy way to say this."

"Then spit it out."

"We're going to have to use the room by the entry as her bedroom."

Faye glanced down at her blueprints. "Are you saying I can't have my salon?"

"Can you think of another room for her to stay? Downstairs?"

Her mind raced, thinking over their layout. "We can set up a bed for her in the living room. Or the playroom. We can convert that. Move the toys upstairs. Or use the sitting room."

"A bedroom right by the front door?" He lifted a brow. "That doesn't offer privacy. That's even worse than the living room because anyone coming in would see it."

"We could put up a barrier. Temporary folding walls. A blanket, even. Actually, that would work even better because then I'd be even closer to her when I'm working. I could easily step away when my clients are under the hair drier or their color is setting. It's a great plan."

Brad frowned.

"You don't think that would work?"

"Her bedroom would be right by the front door."

"It isn't ideal, no. But it isn't the worst plan. And it isn't like it's going to be forever. Right?"

He put his hand on hers. "I hope not, but I can't imagine feeling very welcome having to use a bedroom that's in such a high-traffic area."

Faye rolled up her blueprints and held them close. "It can work. If it doesn't, I don't see how she can stay with us at all. You aren't going to be working from home forever, and if someone needs to be here with her, I'll need my salon here."

He kissed her cheek. "I know this is a big ask, Faye."

Her heart thundered. "You seriously think the junk room is our only option?"

"We can't set up our entry room as a bedroom."

"It isn't the entry. It's a side room and does offer some privacy — especially if you'd listen to my plan of setting up privacy walls. No, it isn't the best solution. That would be the guest room, which is obviously out of the question."

He leaned over to kiss her, but she stood. "I need to check on Hadley. She was napping, but she might be up now and need something."

"Faye, I'm really not trying to stop you from having your dream. I just don't see how it's possible *now*. That's all."

"You're really going to stay home with her?"

"Yes."

"For how long? Kurt's going to need you at the store. The website cover is only going to last so long."

Brad averted his gaze for a moment before rising. "There's something else that needs looking into, and I'm the perfect person for that."

"What?"

"It would appear there's another assassin ring nearby. I need to find out everything I can about that."

Faye nearly dropped the plans. "*Another* one? How close?"

"That's what I need to look into. Don't look so worried."

"You don't think I should be concerned?" Her heart hammered louder than before. "How many killers are nearby? How close are they?"

He put his arms around her. "I'm sure it's nothing to worry about. If they're like the BlueBlade operation, they only go after the bad guys."

Something about his tone shot cold fear through her. "What aren't you telling me?"

His expression tightened.

"Brad." Her hands shook. "We promised to tell each other everything."

"You'd better sit again."

"Just tell me."

"Sit." He pulled out her chair.

She shook her head.

"Please."

They stared each other down, and Faye finally sat. She set the blueprints on the table and wrapped her sweater tighter around her. "What aren't you telling me?"

He frowned and scooted his chair closer to hers. "Someone jumped me the other night when I went to my target."

The chill grew even colder. "Someone tried to kill you?"

"Clearly, they weren't successful. But that isn't my point. He—"

"Someone tried to kill you, and that isn't your *point*?"

He shook his head. "It's what he told me that concerns me."

Faye closed her eyes. "This can't be happening."

Brad took both of her hands. His felt fiery compared to hers. "He didn't hurt me. I'm fine."

Her stomach lurched. She had no words.

"He told me he was working for Wes."

It took a moment for her to put it together. "You're saying that Wes hired him to attack you?"

"To kill me."

She gasped and trembled. "He … he's serious enough about wanting you dead that he would *pay* someone to do it?"

"That isn't even the crazy part. He—"

"Not the crazy part? The man threatened our daughter, and now he's paying people to kill you! We need to call Detective Stewart right now. This needs to stop! It's too much."

"The police can't know about these operations. At least not mine. I don't know what the deal is with the other one, if it's legit or not. That's why I have to spend some time on that. It's going to take some real research, and it needs to be done by someone who's been in the business a long time like I have."

"You have to at least tell the detective that Wes hired someone to kill you."

"While I was on a job myself? He knows what he's doing. It blows my mind that he knew I was out there. Kurt thinks the guy followed me, but that isn't possible. I'm too careful for that."

"I followed you to the prison, and you didn't notice."

"That was different. I wasn't on the lookout for anyone following me — I wasn't hiding anything. My point is, I need to be home to research all of this."

"Mom," Hadley called from upstairs.

"Coming, honey!" Faye stood. "I need you to look up the privacy walls I was telling you about. They'll work. Then we can both be home to keep an eye on her. I want to leave the house even less knowing what you told me about Wes."

"If it makes you feel any better, I did let the detective know about him threatening Hadley and the whispers of his infidelity. She was concerned about that and promised to look into everything and to talk with him about a restraining order."

"What about—"

"Mom!"

Faye headed for the stairs. "We'll talk about this later."

Brad nodded.

"Look into the walls. I'm serious about that. They'll allow me to have my salon *and* her to have privacy."

"Sure."

"I'm serious."

"Okay."

She sighed as she hurried up the stairs and tried to switch gears.

Hadley lay on her bed, still pale but looking better than she had the night before.

"What do you need, honey?"

She pulled some stringy hair from her face. "Can I get more food?"

The plate Faye had brought up an hour earlier was empty.

"You ate that already?" Her spirits lifted.

Hadley nodded. "And I started working on my homework, too."

"Don't worry about that yet. The school knows you were hospitalized. You'll have extra time for everything." Faye picked up the empty plate. "More of the same?"

"Sure."

"Did you think at all about what the doctor said?"

"About what?"

"The procedure."

Hadley sat up straighter. "You all make it sound so sterile, but what you're really suggesting is to have me kill Duke all over again."

"Honey, he's already gone. Going through with this will only make your life even harder than it already is."

"I'm not having any 'procedure.'" She made air quotes.

Faye collected her thoughts. "Are you willing to talk about this with Dr. Trellis?"

"Yeah, but she won't change my mind, either."

"You don't know that."

"And you always tell me I can do whatever I put my mind to."

She never thought *that*, of all things, would come to bite her in the butt. "Some things are more difficult than others, and I don't think you realize everything pregnancy does to a body. I know you think adoption is a possibility, but—"

"Potential option. Mom, you're stressing me out. That doctor said I needed to stay away from anything that would stress me out."

"If you'd be reasonable, this wouldn't upset you." She left with the plate.

Downstairs, Brad was looking at folding walls on his laptop.

"You're actually looking into those?"

He nodded. "I know how important this is to you. I'm still not sure how my mom will feel about it, but we can see what she thinks."

"Thank you." She kissed him before placing the plate in the sink and gathering more food for Hadley.

Movement outside caught her attention. She leaned over the sink for a better look.

"What's going on?" Brad asked.

"It looks like the neighbors are gathering outside."

"Here?"

"No. Down the street. And it looks like there are flashing lights coming from that way."

"Which direction?"

"Toward the Campbells' house."

The chair squeaked on the floor as Brad leaped up. He raced into the hallway.

Faye followed him outside.

The neighbors were heading toward Wes's house.

Her heart jumped into her throat. Could the police be arresting him?

She clasped her hands together and ran out to her lawn. Then down the street, craning her neck to see what was going on. Couldn't quite see the Campbells' house.

Brad put his arm around her shoulders, and they crossed the street. "Look at that."

Wes, cuffed, was being led to a police cruiser by two officers.

Relief flooded Faye.

That was one problem out of their way. They had plenty more, but those would be much easier to deal with. Now Wes wouldn't be a threat to anyone in their family. Hadley wouldn't have to worry about his vague threat about her being sorry, and they wouldn't have to fear for Brad's life.

Not to mention Allison was finally getting the justice she deserved.

His arrest resolved so many of their problems.

Brad kissed the top of her head as they watched the officers shove Wes into the back of the vehicle.

As they drove past, Wes glared at them from behind the barred window.

The neighborhood was safe again.

Chapter Twenty-Eight

BRAD SET down the boxes of his mom's stuff and wandered into his dad's office. Dust was starting to collect — just like in the rest of the house — because of his mom not being there to take care of anything.

They would need to decide whether to sell the house. A decision he didn't like any more than his mom would. But they could barely take care of one home, much less two.

He sat on the chair and spun, looking at everything through his dad's eyes. The man who worked long, hard hours to take care of his family only to be murdered so young.

And the killer was still walking free.

Now that Wes had been charged for Allison's murder and implicated in Duke's, Brad was able to once again focus on his dad's case. Not that he'd ever gotten very far. The cops hadn't, but he had access to newer technology and resources not available to the police.

If anyone was going to solve this cold case, it would be him. It had been a burning desire since the moment Brad found out about his death.

Now was the time to go through this office with a fine-toothed comb. Well, not right this second. He needed to get back home with his mom's things and help her settle into her new room. To his surprise, she'd agreed to stay in the sitting room by the front door. She already knew about Faye's plans to build the salon, and she didn't want to get in the way of that.

Brad didn't know how long that would last. That was no place for a bedroom, and he didn't like asking her to stay there.

Maybe she would be able to move back here into her own house.

But deep down, he knew that wouldn't ever happen. She was too fragile now.

Another option was building a room for her. There was plenty of space in the backyard to add on to the house. And they would already be doing work by building Faye's salon.

He glanced at his dad's picture. The man who had looked so old when Brad was a teenager now looked young — like someone he might be friends with if he were still around.

"What would you do, Dad?"

He waited, as if the old photo could respond. Then he picked up the frame for a closer look.

Clink.

Brad tilted his head and studied the frame. Gave it a little shake.

Clink, clink.

Had a piece broken inside?

He pulled off the back.

A key slid onto the desk.

Brad's heart skipped a beat. A hidden key.

His dad hadn't wanted anyone to find it.

What did it go to? The drawers he and his mom had never been able to open in the desk?

Brad's pulse thrummed in his ears as he tried the middle drawer.

It slid into place. Turned with just the slightest resistance.

He pulled out the drawer, but this time it wasn't empty.

Papers and pens sprawled out across the drawer. He gingerly lifted them to the top of the desk. The bottom of the drawer was higher than it should've been. It was deeper.

Holding his breath, he maneuvered himself in various positions trying to pull the fake bottom up. Finally, it pulled free.

Two brown rectangular boxes took up most of the space. Something else was hiding in the back.

Brad pulled out the biggest box and slid off the top. It was a revolver.

Loaded.

He removed the rounds, replaced the lid, and pulled out the next box.

A BlueBlade knife.

What was he doing with one of those? The company had barely started before his dad's death.

Brad couldn't recall his dad ever talking about or showing him one of those knives.

He put the lid back on and reached back for the last item in the drawer. It was such a tight fit, his arm nearly got stuck. He scraped some skin off.

It was a ledger.

Why lock that up? The weapons made sense — especially with the gun loaded.

Irritation ran through him, thinking about his mom, who had never touched a gun in her life, living in this house all those years so close to a loaded pistol. What had his dad been thinking?

He opened the ledger. The first page had his dad's name written in his penmanship along with some random numbers. They weren't phone numbers or dates, and they didn't make any sense.

Brad flipped the page over.

A list of names and dates. Some had symbols next to them, some were repeated while others had only been used once.

The same thing for the next page and the next. There were more than a dozen filled pages. Names, dates, and symbols. Hundreds of names. Dates ranging for more than a decade.

Then it all suddenly stopped. One name with a single symbol. No date.

He flipped through the rest of the pages — all blank — until he reached the back.

Engraved were five words that turned his blood to ice.

Property of the Slippery Fish.

His dad had been part of the same organization Wes worked for.

Was that what got him murdered?

Chapter Twenty-Nine

HADLEY LAUGHED and waved to Tyler and Maddy as she slammed her locker shut. Despite her health issues and having missed more than a week's worth of rehearsals, she'd nailed her part that day. She'd done better than anyone else, and they'd all been at each rehearsal she'd missed.

It was hard to keep the grin off her face. She'd told her parents she could handle her normal life *and* pregnancy just fine. And she was right. The only real challenge would be wearing looser clothes soon. At least sweater season lasted through the spring most years, and this season wasn't looking like it would be a particularly warm one.

She'd be great. It would all work out. And with any luck, the baby would have Duke's eyes and she could see him again through the baby.

"Life is going just great for you, isn't it?" came an angry male voice from behind.

Hadley whipped around.

Nate stood glaring, his arms crossed.

Her smile faded. "I'm really sorry about your dad."

"Sure you are."

"I am. You lost your mom, and now your dad is in jail."

His eyes narrowed. "But your life is still perfect."

"You know it isn't."

"Miss popular, star of the school play. I hear you're going to run for student body president next year."

"Doesn't mean I'll win. And besides, a lot of people look down on me now that everyone knows about Duke." She didn't add the part about him telling everyone.

His only response was to rake his fingers through his hair, his eyebrows furrowing as he stared at her.

"Where are you staying?"

"You mean because there are no parents at home?"

She nodded.

"We're still at home. My aunt is staying with us for now."

"That's nice."

"Not really. She complains about her commute every day. We'll either have to move to her place or go into foster care. Nice choices, huh? I won't be able to graduate with my class."

Hadley bit her lip. "Maybe you can find someone else to stay with, or even stay at the house. It's just a few months and you're almost eighteen."

His face contorted into an ugly scowl. "And who's going to want to take me on, huh? The son of a killer? People are saying he was involved with Duke's murder, too. My dad wasn't just a wife murderer, but possibly a serial killer."

She looked around for anyone she could join.

The hall was empty.

Hadley twisted a strand of hair. "You're not even related to him. They can't think you'd be dangerous, too."

"Nobody *knows* about the adoptions, remember. Only you."

"Well, I'm not going to say anything. That's not what friends do."

He snorted. "Obviously, I'm not a friend."

She swallowed. "I hope you're able to stay and graduate with everyone."

"Sure you do."

"I do. Why would I want to see you suffer?"

"Maybe because I broke your confidence and spread the word about you sleeping with Duke?"

Hadley held her bag close, feeling for the pocketknife she now always kept hidden but accessible.

"Whatever." He marched away.

She breathed a sigh of relief and started shaking. It was a good thing she didn't actually need to use the weapon, because she'd drop it.

On the way to her car, Mom kept texting her, asking a million questions. Trying to get her to take extra sessions with the therapist.

Hadley started the car and sent her mom a text saying she was still at rehearsal. She didn't want to go home and have to deal with her mom's hovering.

It was suffocating.

Maybe she should do her homework in the car.

A group of cheerleaders and football players were heading her way.

Norah and her group were still giving Hadley the stink-eye every time they saw her, so there was no way she was going to stick around and see if that was them walking toward her.

She left and headed for the library. At least it was quiet there. Unlike school and unlike her house. With so many people plus a dog and a cat, there was never any silence.

Especially with Zeke either yelling at his game or blasting his old-fashioned music.

It was like he wanted people to dislike him.

Her stomach rumbled, and she realized how famished she was. Instead of going to the library, she drove to an all-organic restaurant that kids from school never went to because of the prices.

After scarfing down not just one but two meals, she finally felt better. And she'd been right about kids from school. Other than her, there were just families dining there. Now she could face her homework.

When she was starting her car, she noticed a car way at the end of the parking lot. All the others were, like hers, congregated close to the building.

Curious, Hadley drove toward it. It was hard to see because there were no lights near it.

But when she turned down a row, her headlights shined on it.

Nate's car.

Her heart skipped a beat.

No, it was just a car that *looked* like his. It was crazy to think it was actually his.

She drove closer anyway.

Someone sat in the driver's seat.

A guy. Same hairstyle as Nate's.

Her hand slid off the steering wheel.

He'd really followed her? Now what? He was waiting for her to leave?

Goosebumps ran down her back.

How had she ever thought she could trust him? He was just as crazy and creepy as his dad — regardless of genetics.

She turned sharply and hurried toward the exit.

Nate's car turned and inched toward her, lights off.

Her throat dried. She couldn't swallow.

He knew where she lived, and he had nothing left to lose.

She had to lose him.

And hope he wouldn't decide to wait for her outside her home.

Chapter Thirty

HADLEY TOOK random turns and paid more attention to her rearview mirror than what was in front of her.

Nate was following her. He was staying back behind three other vehicles, but it wasn't enough to stay out of her line of sight.

Somehow, he managed to follow her every turn.

She needed to do something drastic to get away from him.

Hadley hit the gas when a light turned yellow. This time, she actually hoped a cop was there to see her speed through the intersection. Then she could tell him about Nate following her.

No such luck.

She turned left, then right, then left again. Now she was in the neighborhood nearest hers. It wouldn't be impossible for him to find her, but he might think she'd gone home.

All she had to do was wait it out.

Hadley pulled up to a curb behind an RV and cut her lights. She craned her neck, trying to see around the giant vehicle. The best she could hope for was seeing his head-lights if he turned this way.

She focused so hard on trying to see around the RV, she didn't notice the lights behind her until the car was just behind her.

Her heart nearly exploded.

But the pickup truck drove right past her.

Her insides turned to mush. She slid down in the seat and tried to control her breathing.

Once she had her bearings again, she pulled back onto the road and headed for her neighborhood. She'd be better off going home than playing this game.

Much more stress, and she'd be likely to start bleeding again. Although, at least she was eating, resting, and staying hydrated. That would help avoid another hospital trip.

Her phone buzzed with a text. Then another, and another. It continued.

She grabbed it. Eight notifications from her mom.

Hadley: Studying. B home later. I'm fine.

This was all definitely too much. She turned down the music, which wasn't loud, and tried to focus.

If everyone would just leave her alone, she could think. That was all she needed.

The park. It had some great little places to hide from the world. Some of her favorite spots were tucked under the weeping willows. She'd found those as a little girl and always loved them, even as she'd gotten older.

She hurried to the playground, keeping a lookout for Nate's car, and stuffed the only thing she needed into her pocket — the knife. The stupid phone kept going off with notifications, and she couldn't deal with any more of that.

Hadley zipped her jacket up as far as it would go, set her car alarm, looked around, and made her way over to the trees. Everything was so much creepier in the dark. A dog even howled in the distance. It was just a neighborhood pet. Nothing scary. Probably a retriever who licked everyone he met.

She found her favorite tree and nestled into a spot. Her skin was afire and her breathing ragged, but at least she was all alone. Nobody could bother her. It was just her and her thoughts.

A car door slammed not far away.

Hadley grasped the nearest branch. Peeked through the leaves.

Didn't see anyone.

She chastised herself for being so jumpy. The park was in the middle of a neighborhood. Car doors opened and closed all the time. Didn't mean it was Nate.

Footsteps sounded.

Hadley froze, her breath hitched. Her heart thundered so loudly she was sure it would give away her location. She squeezed the branch so hard it made her hand hurt.

The footsteps grew louder. Whoever it was, was in the park.

She moved a few leaves, trying to get a better view.

Louder, closer.

There was no way anyone would find her. Even in the daylight it would've been impossible.

He came into her line of sight. The man — she couldn't tell if it was Nate or some random guy — stopped on the path in front of the play equipment. Looked around. Took a few steps. Walked a little farther.

Hadley's hands shook. She let go of the branch before the rustling leaves caught his attention.

The man sauntered around the climbing toys and stopped once back on the path. He was looking for something.

Or someone.

Hadley glanced behind her. The back of the park went up to fenced yards. She'd be trapped if she ran that way.

There was no way to escape without him seeing her. She could only hide. No other choice.

He spun in a circle and stopped facing not far from her. "I know you're here!"

It was Nate.

Hadley covered her mouth to silence a gasp.

She should've gone home. At least her dad would've been there, and if he wasn't, she'd have the rest of her family to back her up. They could easily send Nate on his way.

Not here.

She was trapped.

"I saw your car, Hadley! We need to talk."

Her pulse drummed in her ears. She'd just have to wait it out. He couldn't check out the entire park in the dark. He'd have to give up at some point.

She patted her pocket where the knife was. That was there as a last resort. Once she waved that in front of him and ordered him to leave her alone, he'd know she meant business. Then she could go home.

"Let's sort this out!" Nate called.

What was there to sort out? He was crazy.

No. He was desperate, on edge. His parents were never coming back home and his aunt was going to move him away his senior year.

And he blamed her for everything.

She should've brought her phone. Then she could've texted her parents or called for help.

Now it was just her and her knife against crazy Nate with nothing to lose.

There was nothing she could do, so wishing she had her phone was pointless.

She needed to get away.

Nate shined a light around. "You may as well come out! I'm going to find you."

Hadley held still. Didn't breathe. Waited for him to turn his back to her.

Then she'd make a run for it. Toward her car or away, it didn't matter. Either way, she could run home. She didn't even care if he destroyed the car.

"Ready or not, here I come!"

Her stomach lurched. She started gagging.

Hadley covered her mouth. She couldn't puke. Not now.

Nate shined the light around in all directions. Called her name.

She leaned against the tree trunk and took labored breaths.

He took the path leading to her.

Hadley pressed her back against the trunk as she watched him.

Nate took slow steps, bouncing the beam of light and calling her name almost in a sing-song voice.

Red hot anger replaced her fear. How dare he come after her like this? It was *his* dad who had killed his mom. He'd probably even been in on Duke's murder. Nate might've even had clues he'd ignored.

This was on *him*.

As the fury coursed through her, Hadley knew what she had to do.

She yanked out her pocketknife. Slid it under her sleeve. Luckily, she was wearing a tight long-sleeved shirt.

Then she stepped out.

Nate jolted.

"Thought you were expecting me."

He stood taller. "I knew you were here. You were stupid to park where you did."

"Maybe I wanted you to find me."

"Why did you hide, then?"

"I startled you, didn't I?"

"All of this is your fault!" He took a step closer.

So did she. "You need to leave me and my family alone. Stop spreading rumors."

"It's all true."

"You were told in confidence!"

"Was I?" he snarled. "Oops."

"Why would you do that? What did I ever do to you?"

"Because you have the perfect life! Nothing ever goes wrong for you. Both of your parents are alive and at home. It isn't fair. It should be your dad in jail, not mine."

"Really? When your dad killed your mom? He's right where he needs to be."

He held up a fist. "Shut your mouth."

"If you touch me, I'm going straight to the police."

"How *dare* you!" He moved around and set his phone on a stump, the light in her eyes.

Hadley moved to the side. "Out of my way. I'm leaving."

Nate stepped in front of her. "You need to face the facts. It was your dad who killed Duke. He knew you two were shacking up next door and he killed him."

She balled her fists. "*Your* dad was cheating with Rose! They probably killed Duke together. You're lucky I don't severely injure you to pay back your dad."

Nate burst into laughter. "That's quite a story! Did your daddy come up with that, or did you make it up all on your own?"

"It doesn't take a genius to pull the facts together.

That's what happened. Your mom probably called him out on it, then he killed her. For all the good that did him."

Nate lunged for her.

She darted out of the way.

His expression contorted into a scowl. "Your dad needs to pay, and the best way to do that is to hurt his whore of a daughter."

Hadley's palm stung as it made contact with his face before she realized what she'd done.

"That all you got?" His nostrils flared as he inched closer. "You think you're so tough? Is that why you think Duke gave you any attention? I'll tell you what he saw in you — you're hot. I'll give you that. But that's the *only* thing you have going for you! The only reason you get the lead parts in the play, because everyone likes looking at you. Everything else sucks! You're as stupid as your dad."

She punched him across the face. His blood got on her hand. She wiped it on her pants. "Shut up!"

Nate grabbed his phone. "I just got that on video! All I have to do is show the cops. You're going to jail for assault."

"You antagonized me!"

He stepped aside and smirked. "Not after I edit that part out."

She whipped out her knife and flicked the blade out. "Want to say that again?"

"Oh, even better!" He aimed his phone at her.

Everything took on a red hue. "Delete all of that!"

Nate pulled the phone away. "Never."

She swung at his arm. Purposefully missed.

"That's some aim you have there."

"It's called a *warning*. Leave me alone!"

"Oh? Look, I'm so scared, I'm shaking." He shook his arm and laughed.

"I'm out of here."

"You aren't going anywhere." He grabbed at her arm.

She aimed the knife at his shoulder, this time intending to draw blood.

He ducked.

The blade dug into his neck. All the way.

Their gazes locked. His eyes widened.

Her mouth gaped. She yanked the knife back.

Blood sprayed out. Splattered onto her face. In her eyes, her mouth.

She spit, wiped her eyes. Dropped the knife.

Nate gurgled. Fell to his knees. Reached for her. Dropped his phone. It bounced under him.

Hadley stared, too horrified to move or speak.

He said something. Blood leaked from his mouth, dripped down. Soaked his jacket from the wound.

Tears stung her eyes. She stared in disbelief. "I didn't mean that! You *moved*!"

Nate fell back onto the ground, his hands grasping his neck. His mouth wavered, but no sound came.

Blood pooled underneath him.

He stopped blinking. Stared at her with nothing behind his eyes. His hands fell from his neck.

Hadley's heart hammered.

She had to do something.

But she didn't know what.

Nate was dead.

She'd killed him.

A Quick Favor...

If you enjoyed this book, please take a moment to write a short review on your favorite online bookstore so other readers can enjoy it, too.

Thanks so much!

About the Authors

Stacy Claflin is a USA Today bestselling thriller author who has published more than 75 novels, including Girl in Trouble and The Perfect Death. She has always been curious about the human mind, and in her quest to learn more, she earned a degree in Psychology. Her favorite course was Abnormal Behavior, which has been useful in writing fiction.

Her love for thrillers goes back to her early childhood when she fell in love with Unsolved Mysteries and America's Most Wanted. When Stacy was five, she got mad at a babysitter who wouldn't let her watch the evening news. These days, she spends her free time listening to true crime podcasts or watching documentaries on the subject.

She has been telling stories for as long as she can remember, and as child would often get into trouble for trying to convince friends her wild tales were true. Now she puts her creativity to better use by writing page-turning stories that leave readers begging for more.

Nolon King writes fast-paced psychological thrillers set in the glitzy world of entertainment's power players with a bold, insightful voice. He's not afraid to explore the darker side of human nature through stories featuring families torn apart by secrets and lies.

Nolon loves to write about big questions and moral

quandaries. How far would you go to cover up an honest mistake? Would you destroy your career to protect your family? How much of your soul would you sell to get the life of your dreams? Would you cheat on your husband to keep your children safe? Would you give in to a stalker's demands to save your marriage?

Also By Nolon King and Stacy Claflin

Dead For Good

Dead For Good

Left For Dead

Dead Of Night

Wake The Dead

Dead For Life

Once Upon A Crime

Once Upon A Crime

Twice Upon A Lie

Three Times a Murder

Stand Alone Novels

Lost and Found

A Simple Kill

Blown

Miserable Lies

Secrets We Keep

Close To Home

Heat To Obsession

Tell Me No Lies

Fade To Black

Interpret correctly and ensure fulfillment.
Their lives are forfeit if she fails.
"The next time we see Winter's Edge,
the next time we stand upon this ledge...
'twill be our last.
And I know without a single doubt,
'tis a truth that I could safely shout...
'twill come too fast."

When Storrm, sister of the Battle Commander and Second in Command of the Dragon Clan, finds herself and her Dragon partner, Mystynn the Green, within the Void separating one side of the Veil from the other, she knows not how they'd gotten there. Suspecting Mystynn of having Blocked her memories of the past winter, she refuses to budge, demanding to know what happened or to return to the fight where they were killed, to try to survive using the Magical Healing they Share.

But Mystynn made a promise and though traveling through the Void takes place in the blink of an eye for those left behind, time has no meaning within, so he is duty-bound to take the time to prove to her that they cannot return afore he can get her to move on Past the Veil. Even fearing she will come to hate him when she learns the truth, he Shares his Memories and they embark on a journey of discovery that begins a full fifty winters afore the Battle for the Dragon Clan.

Many secrets unfold in their travels along the streamline of Memory and Storrm is made privy to astonishing new intel. But once she does learn the truth of the past winter's events, she is faced with the most painful decision of her short span of days. Should they return to the battle that forced them to the Void? Or should they continue through to the Beyond?

Darque Legends Novels by Derrien Relyea:
- Darque Legends: The Black War Begins
- Death of Life
- Search for the Wyrdritch
- Battle of Winter's Edge

Coming Soon:
- The Fangs of Solvyngarr (A Darque Legends novel)

In the works:
- Darque Ages: The High Races Counsel (a prequel series)

You can read some of the epic poetry which inspired the Darque Legends series, get updates on the author's activities and hear her read online at http://www.thedragonwarrior.com.